GUNN CAME BACK

Jed Gunn was a man who disliked trouble, and had stayed away from the Blackford district of Wyoming for six years. But duty took him back there, and he figured that nothing could go wrong during his brief visit. But he hadn't reckoned on the malice of Marissa Coates and the darkness on the night trail back to Montana.

SAM GORT

GUNN CAME BACK

Complete and Unabridged

LINFORD
Leicester

First published in Great Britain in 1988 by
Robert Hale Limited
London

First Linford Edition
published December 1991
by arrangement with
Robert Hale Limited
London

British Library CIP Data

Gort, Sam
  Gunn came back.—Large print ed.—
Linford western library
I. Title
823.914

ISBN 0–7089–7126–1

Published by
F. A. Thorpe (Publishing) Ltd.
Anstey, Leicestershire

Set by Words & Graphics Ltd.
Anstey, Leicestershire
Printed and bound in Great Britain by
T. J. Press (Padstow) Ltd., Padstow, Cornwall

1

THERE was a small moon flying through the rack, but the darkness against the ground was almost total and the light burning atop the land that shouldered to the west was like a beacon. Thus it had always been for Jed Gunn and, despite his underlying apprehension, he felt the joy of coming home. It had been six years, and six years in the life of a man who was still three shy of thirty was a long time.

Gunn's instant of somewhat muted elation sighed away from him. He felt a quiver of response pass through his mount's side. Putting out a hand, he gave the animal a sympathetic pat on the withers. Yes, indeed, his mount felt this awareness of home as much as he, but his own happiness could not register fully when he feared what he

1

might find over yonder. For he had been told, when taking a beer at the long bar up in Billings, that his pa was in a bad way and unlikely to last much longer. Big Frank Bellweather had hinted at cancer, and that dread disease had always been the scourge of the Gunn family. It had nailed uncles Mack and Lemuel a decade ago, and laid final claim to aunt Milly last year. Pa — Bert Gunn — was the last of his family, and it would be a sad thing if the same awful suffering that had afflicted his brothers and sister took him also to the grave.

Seeking the ranch trail, Gunn drifted across the range, and his horse, knowing what he was about, found it for him and picked up the pace without any urging. The brute's nostrils were flaring, and there was almost a dance in its hooves. These were the pastures on which it had run as a colt, and it remembered the stables at the back of the ranch house where it had once been coddled and spent nights of ease. Well, its easy start had led to much harder things, for up in Montana it had known little of luxury, and its days of glory were not about to be repeated now, for the reason why Gunn had fled this, his father's Link B-G ranch, had not, so far as he had been able to learn, gone away in the last six years. This must be a quick visit, and no less swift departure. If the Striker brothers found out that he was around, heaven help him! But they weren't going to find out, and he'd have left this Blackford area of Wyoming and re-entered Montana come sunup. After that he would be safe again, and a brief journey northwards would take him back into places where the Striker boys knew better than to go.

The land tilted upwards, but it was a fairly gentle climb and the horse did not slacken speed. Behind the flat rushing of the breeze, that slice of moon now glimmered in a rough-edged slot of polished blackness, and soon the fall of light touched ridge tiles and the outlines of the ranch house etched their crepe presence at the proud summit of the bench on which Bert Gunn had built his home more than a generation ago.

Reaching the broad acres of flat on top of the terrace, Gunn asserted his mastery just enough to turn his horse off the track that led to the stables and other out-buildings and send it down the one that cut across the ground at the front of the house, where the lamplight which he had earlier seen as a beacon glow now shone out through the parlour window and splashed a pool of oily radiance on the ground where the hitching rail stood.

Riding up to the rail, Gunn drew rein and swung stiffly to the ground, shaking his left leg and then his right — to loosen the kinked muscles of his hips and thighs — and then he secured his horse and looked through the window before him, his gaze picking up a rather plump woman in her late fifties, who was drooping before the fireplace with an expression of despondency on lined and sand-grained features which had once been pretty.

Gwen Coates. Or the Widow Coates now. So that good woman was still doing for pa, such times as he needed her. Gunn's heart went out to the woman. If ever there had been a long-suffering female, Gwen Coates had been her name. Pa ought to have married her ten years ago — ought, indeed, to have married her while they were both still young — but it seemed to his son that Bert Gunn had always been a contrary cuss in his relationships with the fair sex and, so the story went, he had tossed over Gwen one day, after years of courtship, and gone and married the girl who had later become Jed's mother. Of course Gwen, caught on the rebound, had wed Lefty Coates not long afterwards, and that must have appeared to be that, but time had robbed the pair of their respective spouses and thrown them together again during Jed's late teens. All well and good from pa's point of view, but there had been another dimension to the business — one that had concerned Bert's son and Gwen's daughter, Marissa — but Jed always felt a mite guilty about that and tried not to think about it.

Walking up to the front door, Jed put out a hand to let himself into the house, but checked his fingers well short of contact with the latch, realizing that he had become a stranger here; but then it occurred to him that being too diffident might give as much offence as being too forward and, perceiving the right measure of compromise, he first knocked on the door and then opened it, calling: "Mind if I come in? It's Jed!"

There was a brief, listening pause; then Gwen Coates's voice asked sharply: "Who?"

"Jed, Gwen. Jed Gunn."

Apart from a sliver of light that was visible on the left — which, as Gunn was well aware, shone out down the edge of the parlour door — the hall before him was in pitch blackness, and about then he heard a movement deep in that darkness which conveyed the impression that somebody who had previously been standing in the space between the kitchen and the parlour had now begun moving towards him. Then the parlour door opened, and lamplight spilled from it in the shape of a wedge, the tall and perfectly formed shape of a rather sombre-looking but unquestionably beautiful young woman moving into the heart of the radiance and halting there, a hand at her throat as she gazed towards him. "You."

"Marissa?"

"You know very well it's me, Jed Gunn," the girl said stonily, glancing to her right, where the much less elegant figure of her mother had just come into full view on the parlour threshold.

"Dead right," he admitted.

"Come in, Jed," the older woman's voice urged.

Gunn entered the hall, shutting the front door behind him. He walked three paces over the tiled floor, then turned left into the parlour, stepping into a room which seemed little changed since he had been away, except that it had taken on a faded and frayed appearance in terms of the carpets on the floor and the tapestry that covered the armchairs and couch. There were, too, several chips among the ornaments, the whitewash on the ceiling had been turned grey by years of smoke from the fireplace, and mama's portrait over the mantelpiece looked decidedly in need of expert cleaning. Obviously pa had lost interest in domestic appearances; for it could not be lack of money for labour and replacements. All the news that had come to Gunn across the years, concerning the Link B-G, had indicated that the ranch continued to be one of the most prosperous in northern Wyoming.

After his quick glance about him, Gunn turned his full attention to the older woman, who had retreated to the hearth and was standing with her hands clasped under her breastbone, the obvious signs of struggle on her surprised face showing that she was rather at a loss. "I'm not sure this is wise, Jed," she suddenly blurted.

"I'm not sure about it myself," he confessed, conscious of the younger woman stopping at his back as he halted in front of her mother. "I saw Frank Bellweather up in Billings. He was passing through. He told me pa was poorly — very poorly. How bad is it, Gwen?"

Gwen Coates's already crumpled face collapsed still further, her grief unmistakable, and tears began to trickle through the misshapen channels in her leathery cheeks, though no sound of actual weeping issued from her.

"Jed," Marissa said coldly, "your father has passed away. He died three hours ago."

Gunn felt the shock explode over his heart and waves of the awful vibration to go starring to the limits of his nervous system. Keeping his feet solidly placed, he breathed in very slowly and deeply, instinctively holding on to the air once his chest was full; then, after a few seconds of steadying himself inwardly, he breathed out just as slowly and said: "Three hours."

"On the stroke of six," Gwen Coates said brokenly. "The end was sudden. One moment he was there, talking to me, and the next he was gone."

"What was it, Gwen?"

The older woman gestured helplessly.

"Cancer," Marissa said.

"I feared it," Gunn said heavily, craning briefly at the girl. "Did he suffer much?"

"No," Marissa replied. "Doc Thrower had recently poured a phial of laudanum into him. But that was most likely what hastened the finish."

"It was the only kind thing we could do," Gwen Coates choked.

"Maybe," Marissa conceded. "But if it hadn't been for that laudanum, Jed might have seen him alive."

"Perhaps it's better like this," Gunn

10

observed. "He's been dead to me for six years."

"Like others among us?" Marissa inquired bitterly.

"Daughter," Gwen Coates pleaded, "this — this isn't the time or place."

"It's both," Gunn said shortly. "Let her say what she wants. There may not come another chance."

"You let me down, Jed," the girl accused.

"What do you care now, Marissa?" her mother demanded. "You've found another man — one you like better. No trouble, please."

"I don't care," Marissa said implacably. "He promised."

"I did," Gunn acknowledged grimly. "I said I'd send for you, in that note I left. And I might have done, if I'd honoured my word. It went well enough for that. But you wouldn't have wanted the life it would have meant. You wouldn't have wanted to be the wife of an odd-jobbing ranch hand."

"You didn't give me the chance, Jed!" the girl fired.

Gunn turned and faced her. He looked deep into the dark brown eyes that had locked upon his own. In her stare he felt an unforgiving strength that made him shiver. Her beauty drew him, but her presence repelled. He sensed an old bitterness which had become a revengeful hatred. He feared that this girl could be actually dangerous, and this daunting awareness transmuted his sense of guilt into the defensive resentment of one who felt himself far too harshly judged. "Now look here, Marissa," he said flatly, "we both of us know just how far it really went. It was a boy and girl affair. There was no more to it than kisses and castles in the air. I did promise to send for you, and I didn't do it. To that extent, I am at fault, and I humbly apologise; but let's not let it get all out of proportion. For me everything changed overnight. I went from boy to man in twenty-four hours. Had to, by cracky!

If I hadn't ridden north, the Strikers would have murdered me, and who to stop them? What good ever was the law in Blackford?"

"Coward!"

Clenching his fists more and more tightly at his sides, Gunn swallowed the word. "Yes," he said as reasonably as he could, "I've asked myself about that. Maybe I was a coward, and it could be I still am. Certainly, at the time of day you're thinking of, I wouldn't have stood a chance against even Zeb Striker — and he's by far the least of those four bad brothers. Yes, Marissa, I could have done the brave thing — stood my ground and got killed — but what good would it have done you, me, or anybody else?" He paused, pale faced and openly angry now. "Go on, girl — tell me!"

"I'd have had a grave to dance on," Marissa answered, smiling her contempt. "So the years have gone. What will you do next?"

He blinked. "I don't get you."

"Your father had one son, Jed," Gwen Coates reminded. "You are that son. This ranch is now yours. I know Bert willed it so."

Gunn hadn't thought in terms of being the heir to the Link B-G ranch in many a day, but now he was confronted by the fact of it. The visions that came numbed parts of him and chilled others, and he perceived that Marissa had recently been thinking of a cowardice other than the physical sort. He didn't want the ranch; it represented too great a burden. He had a life up in Montana that he had made. Oh, it wasn't great, but it was good enough. To stay here, perched above his inheritance, would mean a fight — not only with his own nature but with the Strikers — and who wanted that kind of existence, perhaps for the rest of his days? "I shall sell up," he said.

"No!" Gwen Coates protested. "You mustn't do that, Jed. Think of what your father put into this ranch. All he had — his very life and soul! You can't run away from your responsibilities, son. Your papa told me he hoped you'd come back and take over once he was dead."

"But not while he was living," Gunn commented cynically. "You have to understand this, Gwen. My pa was as scared of the Strikers as Marissa figures I was and am. He encouraged me to ride north in the first place, and advised me not to come back. My reappearance, he warned, could only bring trouble on him and the ranch. Okay, I offended the Strikers, without meaning to — and I don't blame anybody for that but myself — but, while I don't doubt that pa loved me after his fashion, he wanted me out of the way while it suited his purpose, and now I aim to stay away."

"Don't wriggle, Jed," the older woman said severely. "There's wickedness in that decision; and it's a wicked waste too. Only the Striker brothers stand between you and a happy successful life here. You must stand up to them, son!" She threw her daughter a glum, watchful little glance that was somehow significant. "Those Striker boys are only human beings — flesh and blood, like the rest of us! You've got a crew on this ranch, all good men and true, and they'll fight for you like lions, if you ask them. What have you got in Montana that matters so much?"

"Work that's about as regular as I want," Gunn replied. "A few friends to yarn with round the fire. Saturday evenings free. The odd girl who can just about stand the sight of my face. There is a name for it, Gwen. Maybe two. Freedom and peace of mind."

"You're a waster, Jed!" Marissa jeered. "A waster — and a coward!"

Now Gwen Coates shook her head in an exasperation that became capitulation. "I don't know, Marissa. Those words pre-empt God. Bert Gunn was one man; his son is another. Jed may be the wiser of the two. Each to his values while living — because it all comes to much the same thing in the end. Those

16

men of old have much to answer for. They still haunt us from generation to generation with their ill-omened talk of sloth and the burning. Do we know what we were put here for? Anyhow, it's Jed's life, daughter. I've said all I mean to say, and I think you have likewise."

"As the father betrayed you, mother," Marissa said vindictively, "so the son betrayed me, and no words will ever alter that."

"Grow up, girl!" Gunn flashed at her, angered clean out of himself by her unflagging malevolence.

Marissa started back from him, as if she feared that he might slap her, but the look she gave him was a terrible one, and he felt its sheer hatred pierce his solar plexus like the head of an arrow. Then, spinning away from him, the girl returned to the darkness of the hall, her left turn and the recession of her footfalls suggesting that she was bound for the kitchen.

"I'm sorry, Jed," her mother said.

"She went too far. I wish I hadn't brought her with me."

"Forget it!" he urged. "You weren't to know I'd appear. Besides, it's better out than in."

"There's that," Gwen Coates conceded. "I expect — you'd like to see him?"

"I guess so," Gunn answered, the fingers of his left hand lightly pressed to where the girl had stabbed him with her hatred. "He was my father."

"We are as we're made," the woman reminded sagely, turning from the hearth and making for a door in the wall on the right of the fireplace. "According to his lights, I don't suppose Bert Gunn was much better or worse than the rest of us."

"I can see you loved him, Gwen," Gunn said, moving towards the spot where she now stood with her hand upon the latch. "He was lucky in that."

Opening the door, the woman glanced over the tip of her right shoulder, frowning slightly. "Love?" she queried.

18

"I wish you could tell me what that is, Jed. He gave me a reason for living. But there were days when we squabbled like cat and dog."

"That's love sure enough," Gunn said wryly, treading in her wake as they entered the room behind the door.

"Over here, Jed."

Gunn slowed as she walked up to a big brass bedstead that stood with its head against the wall on their left. A table had been positioned at the further side of the bed, and upon it burned an oil lamp that had three globes of figured glass. On the bed itself, oddly small when compared with the dimensions of memory, lay a human shape which was shrouded by the bedclothes, and now Mrs Coates turned back the top sheet and counterpane, revealing the utterly motionless and badly shrunken features of Bert Gunn, his eyes weighted with dollar coins and his jaw held firmly in position by a handkerchief that passed round the sides of his head and was tied on top of his crown.

Leaving the head and shoulders of the corpse uncovered, Gwen Coates retreated to the foot of the bed and stood with her hands upon the rail while Gunn closed in and looked down on the fleshless caricature of his once supremely vigorous two-hundred and twenty pound parent, shuddering inwardly at the ravages which cancer had wrought on a neck that had worn a size eighteen collar in its prime and shoulders that had measured twenty-four inches across them. "Poor old guy," he said, thinking back to that day when he had managed to give the hunting Strikers the slip and gallop back here for provisions and a blanket-roll before hastening north — with something less than his father's blessing. "I guess you couldn't blame him for how he took my trouble. After ma died, this ranch *was* everything to him, and he must have found my ways a sore disappointment. I suppose the truth is, I preferred poking around the hills on horseback to hard work. Well, whatever he felt, it's all over now — God rest him."

"Amen."

"And spare us."

"Both," Gwen Coates emphasized.

"Amen to that," Gunn said fervently, turning away from the body and moving aside so that Gwen Coates could leave the foot of the bed and shroud the remains once more. "I expect Wally Allen will take care of the burying."

"Yes," the woman said, quickly doing her work and making little noise about it. "You needn't concern yourself with the funeral. I'll see the undertaker."

"Thank you."

"I can see you want to get away."

"Safest for everybody," he agreed, failing to completely keep the cynicism out of his voice. "Most especially me — naturally."

"Won't you let me get you a meal first?" Gwen Coates asked, walking behind him as he moved out of the death room. "You must have time for that."

"No," he said, going to the fireplace in the parlour and holding his hands to the flames. "All I want to do is make my peace with that girl of yours. She tried me, but I ought not to have snapped at her as I did."

"I think she deserved it," Mrs Coates said; "but you know how you feel about it."

He turned to where the woman now stood beside the oaken table at the centre of the living room. "Please call her, Gwen."

Nodding, the woman walked to the door that led into the hall. "Marissa!"

There was no answer.

"Marissa!"

There was still no reply.

Gwen Coates gave a small mutter of irritation, as if she suspected that her daughter was being awkward; then, seeming to cast off her normally flesh-burdened walk, she stepped out into the hall with a young woman's lightness of foot and passed quickly through the blackness there into the rear of the house. Apparently in the kitchen now, she called her daughter's name again, once more without reply; then, after sounds which suggested that she had opened the back door and looked outside, she made a hurried return to the parlour, saying: "I'm afraid she must have gone home, Jed. Certainly her horse is no longer at the kitchen hitching post. I'll tell her that you wanted to say sorry when I see her again."

"No," Gunn said with abrupt decision. "Let it go, Gwen. Might be better if I kept my pride. I guess Marissa isn't the kind of girl a man apologises to. She'd only take it for a sign of weakness." He chuckled harshly to himself. "For all she hates my innards, it seems she hasn't been put off men. Who's the fellow sparking her?"

"Now Jed," the woman chided, putting on a smile to hide what could have been the wariness that she had inadvertently displayed, "that's none of your business. You're not the kind of man who goes prying into a girl's love life, are you?"

"No, ma'am!" he assured her. "Couldn't see the harm in asking, that's all." Then he nodded to himself with finality. "I can't think of anything else. Visit over. I guess I'll hit the trail."

"Let me kiss you farewell, Jed."

The woman approached him. Grinning faintly, he bowed his more than six feet until his face was at a height that she could easily reach. He let her kiss him on the left cheek, then straightened up again, giving the top of her right arm a small squeeze. "Thanks, Gwen."

"Jed, with all your faults, you'd have made much the better son-in-law."

"I'll remember those words," he promised, craning a moment as he headed for the hall and the front door. And so he would; but he was already asking himself what exactly she had meant by them.

2

GUNN stepped out into the night, shutting the front door of the ranch house behind him. He faced the hitching rail, and his horse snorted at him disappointedly. Walking towards the animal, he muttered a soothing word; then stiffened as he heard a movement at his back and dropped his right hand to his holster, spinning to glimpse a man's shape emerging from behind the front corner of the house nearest to him. "Who is it?" he asked tightly.

"It's John Dingle, Jed."

"John." Dingle was the Link B-G's foreman, and a friend of Gunn's formative years. "How did you know I was here?"

"Had a hunch the boss's condition would bring you home sooner or later," the foreman explained. "Bad

25

news travels fast."

"That's a most remarkable intuition you have, John," Gunn said dryly. "Have you been waiting around for a month or two?"

"No," Dingle said. "Got it from Marissa Coates you were here. I was out at the big corral, enjoying a smoke, when that girl came stamping out of the kitchen fit to split herself and went to her horse."

"Marissa and I had had a spat," Gunn said.

"It didn't take much working out," the foreman remarked. "You want to steer clear of that filly."

"Why?"

"She's thick with the Strikers," Dingle answered. "She's Alec's girl."

Gunn whispered softly to himself, then muttered something blasphemous. No wonder Gwen Coates had made that remark concerning sons-in-law just now. Though she most probably lacked the innocence of Little Red Ridinghood, Marissa had undoubtedly fallen victim to the Big Bad Wolf himself. It wasn't to be wondered that the mother was rather fearful for her daughter. If there was a crime that Alec hadn't committed, it must be the one that Satan was keeping to himself. Killer, thief, bully, lecher — he was all of them, and several more. Now a man in his late thirties, he had taken and discarded dozens of women across the years, and it was unlikely that Marissa would ultimately fare any better than the rest. "Fool of a girl!"

"Alec's girl," Dingle said pointedly — "and your enemy."

Catching his breath as he picked up the significance of the foreman's words, Gunn pondered it for a moment or two and then let it go. "No," he said confidently, "she wouldn't do a thing like that."

"For you to say," Dingle returned doubtfully. "But that's not why I'm here. You can guess why I am, I expect."

"Friendship and condolences, I hoped."

"Yes, those — and something else."

"The ranch?"

"That's it."

"Figures Marissa talked plenty."

"I wouldn't have called her all that complimentary either."

"Get to the gist of it."

"She said you aimed to sell up."

"I hadn't expected to be faced with it," Gunn confessed, slightly on the defensive but also wishing to be completely honest about it. "I don't see that it's anybody's damned business but mine — but, yes, I do intend to sell up. I know a ranch valuer and land agent up in Billings, name of Blow, and I'll be sending him down here shortly to value the place and prepare a sale."

"It's your ranch," Dingle conceded, "and you have the right to dispose of it how you wish. But you've got a score of men in the bunkhouse who're looking to you for their livings. They're ready to fight for you, Jed. Or are you *that* afraid of the Strikers?"

"I'm going to take that as an honest

question, John," Gunn said crisply, "and answer it in the same way. Yes, I'm afraid of the Strikers, but not so afraid that I would not fight them if I had to. Point is, mister, I don't have to; and, much as I may appreciate the willingness of the hands to fight my fight, I can't risk their lives against four of the most skilled and ruthless killers in the Northwest. Apart from anything else, I feel I owe that as a duty to my late pa. He always thought first of the health and safety of his men."

"That's true, Jed," Dingle acknowledged, "and the crew and I held your father in great respect because of it. But sometimes you've got to fight, Jed. There's an unwritten law in the cow country. A hired man shall fight for the brand. Me and the boys live by that law. We also accept that every man has his appointed day and hour, and there's nothing we can do to change it."

"More a matter of faith than fact, John," Gunn observed. "My heart wouldn't be in it. I've never had any wish to be a boss-man and order the lives of other men. I value my freedom, and I like the simple life. I guess I'm just another cowboy at heart, and I belong more in the bunkhouse than the master bedroom."

"You got the wrong start," Dingle said. "Your pa didn't take the trouble to train you. I guess he had too much else on his plate. When trouble struck, he encouraged you to run for it, and I suppose you've kept running. I'm disappointed, Jed, and it's no good saying I'm not. The boys will be disappointed too."

"I wish I didn't know what they're feeling," Gunn growled. "It's not that I haven't been in the same position. I had to piece up myself when that English cattle company, Richmond Beef Incorporated, went bust. It hurt. We had fair billets with those limejuicers." Then he saw a possible answer, and came to another abrupt decision. "Are you ready to consider a kind of compromise, John?"

"Depends on what you mean, Jed."

"Tell you how we could work it," Gunn pursued. "I'll name you my manager here, and make the necessary legal and financial arrangements for you to run the Link B-G. That way I can take a slice, you can be boss, and the men will keep their jobs. What do you say?"

"No," Dingle responded. "Not because I don't want what you offer, but because I'm not up to it. It's not a thing a man wants to boast about, Jed, but I finished school at eleven years. In the second grade. I can sign my name, count, and read simple things; but by no stretch do I have the education necessary to manage a ranch of this size. Why, your pa spent a whole day every week, just writing."

"I respect your judgement," Gunn said. "So that's knocked that on the head then. I'll see Pete Blow as soon as I can. He ought to get down here by the end of the week. I'll ask him to organize a sale that's as quick and painless as possible. Mean time, I'll make sure you and the men go on getting your pay through the Central and Northwestern Bank. I can attend to that business in Billings."

"Don't be too hasty, Jed," Dingle pleaded. "Give yourself a week or so think it over. If only because the Link B-G is a healthy, going concern which serves the country as well as the folk who work it. It isn't a sickly business that deserves to be pole-axed. That would be butchery." Changing feet in the darkness, and almost invisible of face, he made a number of small tut-tutting sounds that expressed both frustration and anxiety. "Wouldn't it then? Wouldn't it? Come on now!"

Gunn didn't like the manner in which this was developing. Time was slipping, and he wanted desperately to get away. Dingle, normally a withdrawn and taciturn man, was in danger of becoming downright importunate. Gunn simply could not let the other lower himself that far. "Okay, John," he said quietly — "okay. I had spoken my last word, and it's as well you know it, but I'll promise to think it over." He released a harsh and regretful breath. "Not that I think it will make the slightest difference. Now fare-you-well, my friend, and please pass my respects to all in the bunkhouse."

Turning from the foreman, Gunn went to his horse and, untying it, mounted up and drew its head round. Then, hearing Dingle speak a disconsolate "so long", he followed the path away from the house and soon came to its union with the home trail. Here he turned right and began descending the eastern face of the bench, bearing left when he reached the bottom and kicking for a trot as he prepared to quarter away from the eminence on which the ranch house sat and pick up the Yellowstone Trail that had brought him down from the north and would take him back again. He planned to make a steady ride of it up to Belfry and there break his journey back to

Laurel and Abel Whittaker's Silver Tips ranch, where he was currently putting in his time. Say, eighteen miles to Belfry. He ought to be able to do it in three hours. True, his mount had been on the go since noon, but it should be able to stand another reasonable spell of travel without showing signs of being overworked.

The night closed upon Gunn and the horse, and the feelings of familiarity thinned away to nothing. The brute loped steadily towards the Montana line, its hoofbeats echoing dully. Saddened by events, as he inevitably was, Gunn felt the additional mental burden of a dropping atmospheric pressure, and he thought it might rain before long. He kept seeing his father's dead face — and his mother's also, dimmer but still plain — and, haunted by the past, he deliberately shifted his mind from the ghostly visages and began reliving the events which had turned the brothers Striker into his enemies.

It had all begun in the town of

Blackford. With a beer or two inside him, he had stopped outside the law office and passed an eye over the Wanted posters pinned on the notice board. There had been that one of Mort Weir, an old style woodcut that enhanced the blemishes. Pudgy-cheeked, broken-nosed, slate-eyed, hog-skulled and totally bald, Weir, hanged two years ago in Rapid City, had been a character, even among the rough tough desperadoes of his day, and he could not have been mistaken by any man with even half an eye. Thus it had been one hell of a shock when, only minutes after looking at Weir's likeness — and not more than a mile out of town — Gunn had met the badman at a crossroads. Weir, riding a hammerheaded coyote swayback that was as ugly as himself, had shown complete disinterest in the younger man, and crossed Gunn's path, heading west.

After riding on for a bit and assimilating his surprise, Gunn — not without thoughts of playing the hero in Weir's capture — had decided to turn back and dog the outlaw's tracks, purposing to pinpoint his next stopping place, then return to Blackford and report the position of the man's camp to Sheriff Buck Lammas.

It had been an absorbing piece of tracking, and Gunn had barely given it a thought when he had passed onto Striker land. Using the country to full advantage, he had shadowed Weir into the high rock at the back of the Striker grass and found himself among the cliffs and ridges that enclosed the legendary Eagle Valley, which was said to be impenetrable to all but trained mountaineers.

There had been this stream, and then that tunnel through a hill of stone. Weir had entered the tunnel and, after giving it a minute for safety's sake, Gunn had pursued. He had ridden through the whole length of the tunnel — which had proved about a quarter of a mile long — and emerged in what amounted to a short valley. The stone wall on the left met the water itself, but there was a well-grassed bank on the right that extended between the stream and the apparently imprisoning cliff on that side. Directly ahead was another bluff, broken along its base, and here the waters went underground in such limiting circumstances that no man could possibly travel with them further. Thus Gunn ought to have come upon his quarry in the forty-odd yards of rock-confined space before him, but in fact there was no trace of the outlaw in the boxed area.

Gunn recalled reining in at the stream's centre. He had looked around him anxiously for indications of where the badman might have gone, and decided that he could only have left the water on the right. Turning his horse, Gunn had climbed it out of the stream on that side and begun to examine the bank there, finding fresh sign that led across the grass and up to a considerable patch of greenery that masked a portion of the valley wall adjacent.

Probing now, Gunn had discovered almost at once that the greenery concealed the presence of a big rift in the boundary rock that penetrated for fifty yards into the rear of what could only be Eagle Valley. But these details, interesting enough on reflection, had failed to take on importance at the time, for Gunn had immediately spotted a trio of horsemen lounging astride their horses in the gap. He had identified the men as Mort Weir and Alec and Colin Striker, and the three had been laughing and talking together in the friendliest of manners, the sight suggesting that Weir had been expected at this secret spot and that Alec and Colin Striker had been on hand to greet him.

Unfortunately, diverted though he was, Alec had not so far lost his sense of caution as to fail to glimpse Jed's face peering along the rift at him and his companions. Yelling in fury, the senior of the brothers Striker had declared that he knew the spy's name and Jed Gunn was as good as dead. Then the

Colts had started to bang, and Gunn, realizing that he must either beat the fastest possible retreat or remain here as the occupant of an unknown grave, had climbed his horse about and sent it surging back into the stream, his mad gallop after that carrying him back through the tunnel that pierced the hill of stone.

He had left the water at the first moment he could on the further side of the rock mass, then angled back into the grassland to the east, pretending that Blackford was his goal. In fact he had wanted only to reach the Link B-G which adjoined the Striker range at one point — and, hiding when he had seen his opportunity, let the chase go galloping by him and then doubled round and headed for home, where he had told his father what had happened and been confirmed in his own intention to grab some gear and head north into Montana — where Gunn senior had believed that the Strikers had prices on their heads and this he had done, taking certain suspicions with him, and thus the pattern of a rather aimless life had been broken and reassembled in another form of aimlessness which had become the way of the grown man.

But, though Gunn was determined to persist in it, he was aware right now that he was less happy than he believed. He was conscious of the man within himself whom he often suppressed, and had no doubt of strengths and abilities that could still achieve more if he put them to work. But who lived a perfect life? Who, indeed, was allowed to live a perfect life? The world was a jungle, and the strong were always seeking goods and the power to rule. They brushed aside those who stood in their path. Gunn sensed that Nature had equipped him to play the ruthless fellow with the worst of his generation, but he shied away from the very thought, for he knew that there could be neither peace nor happiness in harrying those of a weaker mould.

Increasingly weighed down by feelings of grief and being at cross-purposes with everything that had kept him on the level until now, Gunn again went back to the atmospheres of six years ago and wondered if his life could be on the brink of another enforced change, and an indefinable sense of dread built up in him as he gazed into the formless vistas of a future over which he might have little control. His spirits had travelled far down this irrational path, when he was alerted by some part of himself to presences in the surrounding darkness and his hand went once more to his revolver. Then something thin but unyielding caught at him beneath the chin and plucked him out of the saddle, and he struck the ground so heavily that all the air was knocked out of his lungs and his senses went reeling through an inner firmament.

Lying spreadeagled on the trail, he became slowly aware of those presences, earlier sensed, closing upon him, and

41

then glimpsed faces above his own as strong hands gripped his clothing and roughly sat him up. After that a match flared, and the flame was pushed into his face, its sulphurous stink getting into Gunn's throat and making him cough. Then a male voice that was gruff and full of cruelty said: "It's him, Alec."

"Didn't see who else it could be, Colin," drawled the voice of a second man. "But you never can tell. There never was a night yet that didn't have its travellers." He paused. "Right. Let's get this organized. Zeb, bind his hands behind his back. Dan, you hold your gun against his head. Scatter his brains if he so much as draws an uneven breath."

Gunn felt the muzzle of a revolver grind into the left side of his skull, and the double clicks of a smoothly cocking hammer went ringing through his head like blows struck on an anvil. The match went out, and the night seemed darker than death. Now his hands were yanked behind his back, and a noosed leather thong was passed over his fingers and pulled tight about his wrists. After that a number of knots were tied to ensure that his arms were fully secured behind his back. "Know who we are?" demanded the second of the two voices that Gunn had heard speak, the one that had been giving the orders.

"Knew by the smell of you from the first moment," Gunn replied defiantly. "May heaven's curse follow Marissa Coates! Only a woman would do what she's done to me."

"I'll tell her what you said," Alec Striker promised, abruptly delivering a kick between the prisoner's legs.

Screaming in agony, Gunn folded over his knee caps and, the sweat trickling down his temples as he fought back further shrieks of suffering, he forced himself to begin quenching the awful pains that filled his pelvic basin.

"That'll teach you to watch your manners, Gunn," Alec Striker said.

"We bathe as often as you do. They say cleanliness is next to Godliness. I reckon you're the kind of fellow who would believe that nonsense." He flicked the captive's right ear. "Are you a praying man, Gunn?"

"I pray, Striker."

"Then get on your feet and start praying now!" the other commanded. "You'll have just long enough to make your peace with heaven while we're walking you to the tree we've got picked out for you to decorate."

Gunn tried to move his legs, but could not. The whole of his lower body was paralysed. He literally could not have stood up to save his life.

"He's crippled!" a porky voice giggled. "Should you have kicked him there, Alec? Them gals in hell will have to go short. Ain't right, y'know. Them poor bitches ain't got much else to look forward to. Haw, haw, haw!"

"Hold your row, you fat fool!" Alec Striker ordered disgustedly. "How did us three stalwarts come to get stuck with a wet article like you for a brother?"

"How'd I come to get stuck with you three?" came the surly rejoinder. "So I ain't one o' Pharaoh's lean kine. That don't mean I ain't got feelings like other folk."

"Tell us about it tomorrow," Alec advised coldly, "and pick that bastard up. His lynching is six years overdue. I want to hear that rope creaking as he kicks and twists in the night wind."

A pair of thick arms closed about Gunn's upper body. He felt himself heaved to the vertical and then held there as his knees at once threatened to buckle under him. "Aw, be a man, Jed!" begged the fat individual holding him up.

Gunn did his best to oblige. The muscles of his face gathered as he squeezed small the pain that was still afflicting him and, setting his feet apart, he held himself firmly erect, shaking off the support that he was still receiving from the rear. Then the muzzle of the pistol ground once more into the soft tissue behind his left temple. "March!" ordered a fourth voice, which could only belong to Dan, the Striker brother who had not previously spoken.

Putting one foot unsteadily before the other, Gunn moved slowly to the front, each step costing him more than words could tell; but, as his agonies intensified again, so his mind confused, and his awareness of reality was at least blunted to the terrible ordeal that could lie only minutes away. Indeed, he felt more dead than alive as his almost blind progress was halted and he heard the movement of boughs above him and the uneasy snorting of horses from nearby on his right.

"I want this done properly," Alec Striker said with authority. "I told you to bring a lantern, Colin. Did you?"

"It's there," his brother Colin answered — "on my saddle."

"Fetch it," Alec snapped, "and the rope."

Colin Striker's very tall and slightly stooping shape left the group under the tree. His footfalls moved in the direction of the horses. He was away for about half a minute, then returned and struck a match, his lean, fine-boned face springing into view like that of a handsome but irredeemably wicked fiend's. In his left hand he carried a storm lantern, and he raised the glass on this and touched off the wick, bringing a circle of dull but adequate light to the grass under the mountain oak which was to serve as the hanging tree. After that, handing the light to Zeb of the fat belly, he slipped off the lariat which he had hung across his upper body and, looking up now at a thick bough which jutted from the tree's main division about eight feet above the ground, shook out the noose and cast the rope upwards, its end sailing over the bough and falling just far enough to leave the loop hanging at the level of a six-foot man's shoulder.

"She'll do, son," the wide-shouldered and hook nosed Alec approved, a hellish glitter in the deep set eyes that he turned on the prisoner. "Have you done praying, Gunn?"

"Get on with it," Gunn advised as bravely as he could, hearing his own voice as if it belonged to somebody else.

"Now that's real accommodating of you, Mr Gunn," Alec Striker sneered, gesturing at the bull necked, gimlet-eyed man who still had his gun clapped to the prisoner's head. "To me, Dan."

Dan Striker forced Gunn under the limb of the tree from which the lariat hung, stopping him at a position convenient to the rope and Alec's reach. Then Alec shaped the noose anew and dropped it over Gunn's head, jerking it tight and saying: "Zeb, Colin — gimme a hand!"

The part of the rope still coiled was quickly unwound, and Alec and the two brothers named took up positions on the slack and pulled just hard enough to bring their victim's jaw level. Gunn choked slightly and gazed into the gloom before him, unable to credit that any of this was really happening to him. He told himself that he would wake up at any moment now — probably with a headache, a foul taste in his mouth, and the knowledge that he had been on the booze — but he didn't wake up, and the tree stirred above him in the wind, its old leaves rattling in a kind of glassy menace that told him to prepare.

Then Alec Striker spoke the word. The three hangmen heaved with all their strength, and the noose grabbed at Gunn's throat, cutting deeply, then carrying him off the ground and upwards, until he simply hung there, toes struggling in his boots after the security of a ground that he could no longer feel. Abruptly conscious that he was now unable to draw breath, the panic hit him, and he started to kick, the rope above him beginning to creak out the hideous song that Alec Striker had so wished to hear.

He felt it starting to happen. His eyes popped, and his tongue bulged out of his mouth. He entered a red hell of suffering. His chest and skull seemed to slowly inflate to bursting point, and an ammunition dump exploded in his brain, casting starry fire in all directions. The lights turned a vivid scarlet, and their background grew blacker and blacker, thought fragmenting and sense passing away. Then he ceased to feel his body, and everything became a blank.

3

GUNN had always understood that the dead awoke in a brighter and better place. But, as he opened his eyes and peered mistily around him, the one in which he now found himself seemed even poorer and more gloomy than the one he had left. Still, he must be fair about it; he hadn't lived without sin; and it was likely that the good angels had kicked him downstairs and that he was presently recovering from the pangs of death in an anteroom of hell. Doubtless there would be an interview with the Evil One shortly, and it would be decided to what use the netherworld could put his dubious talents. He could see himself coming out of this with a stoker's job. Old Sam Betts had always declared that he was a master hand with a shovel.

Trouble was, he didn't feel dead as

he had always expected to feel dead. In fact he still felt remarkably alive what between the hurting in his throat and the pain that remained present between his legs — and, as a fury towards the Striker brothers gathered in him, he began to feel good and sure that, if they didn't batten down the door, he'd be hopping out of hell very soon and going off to haunt those long varmints into their graves. And when they got to the Pit, let them look out anew. But that could well prove to be what His Satanic Majesty had in mind as one of those torturous diversions with which he regaled himself as the expense of earth's wicked.

He was suddenly aware of a woman's shape coming between him and what light there was. "Are you all right, Jed?" a contralto voice asked. "I haven't made a mistake, have I? You are Jed Gunn, aren't you?"

"You have to ask?" he mumbled thickly.

"Well, it has been a number of years,"

the female said defensively.

"Figures you keep the Record Book down here," Gunn croaked, glimpsing the woman's face and deciding that it was beautiful in that firm-lipped, sad-eyed mould which he had always admired. "Old Nick give you the job? I'd have expected him to pick somebody with a better memory than you've got. But then I guess we're all second class folk down here."

"Down here?" the woman inquired bemusedly. "What are you running on about?"

"You can't expect a newly dead man to have perfect control of his tongue!" Gunn protested. "I am dead, aren't I?"

"Not unless I am too," the woman answered, beginning to laugh — "and I'm very sure I wasn't a few minutes ago when I lifted you in here on my back."

"How can it be possible?" Gunn demanded. "Those men lynched me."

"Not quite," the woman said, stepping back to a spot where the light from an oil lamp that burned on top of a small wooden table at the middle of the room could play upon her brown-skirted and check-shirted figure. "They left you hanging there those vital seconds too soon. I was able to cut you down and revive you. It was touch and go, but the spark was still there, and I soon fanned it back to flame."

"Golly Moses!" he breathed, looking close about him and seeing that he lay on a frame bed that had no mattress and precious few items of linen. "It must have been a near thing!"

"I doubt it could have been closer," she acknowledged. "Forget about it, Jed. Just rest."

"Forget about a miracle? I can't."

"You could say everything that really mattered was in your favour," she sighed. "I heard you all, and happened to be nearby when they lighted their lantern. I hid myself in the bushes only yards away from that oak. I had my sharpest knife with me, and I managed to reach the rope from which you hung in a trice, by jumping up. I slashed, and down you came. And thus I was able to start blowing air into your lungs — as my father once taught me long ago — with a minimum of delay."

"There's no question that you saved my life," Gunn said, gasping with pain as he sat up and began gingerly massaging his throat with the fingertips of both hands. "I know you, don't I? We were at school together. We used to sort of look at one another now and again across the class."

"That's right," she agreed. "I was a little girl then, and you were one of the big boys."

"Seems to me you're a big girl now," he commented, and so she unquestionably was; for she was nearly six-feet tall, honey-blonde, blue-eyed, and built like an Amazon. "Grace." He frowned, suddenly remembering that thing about her that was best forgotten. "Grace Tucker."

"Yes," she sighed. "Oh, you men!"

"The Strikers wronged you too."

"Just before you fled the district," she agreed. "My mother was still alive then. What those four devils did to me was the death of her. That — and what came out of it."

"Came out of it?" he prompted.

"I had a child," she explained bitterly. "One of those four brothers was the father of it. They all raped me through an afternoon and evening. Then they stripped me naked and whipped me home to Blackford. It was a disgrace. I was disgraced in the eyes of the whole town. The Strikers declared I was all for what happened. Mother became ill of shame, and we were obliged to move out here into the woods — into this old trapper's hut — because Blackford wouldn't have us. As I grew big with child, so mama's sickness grew worse. Then she died, and I had to bury her — out here in the forest."

"Obviously I knew the part of the story that I could know," Gunn said. "It was no fault of yours, Grace. It

56

was an experience forced on you. Every right-thinking person knew it. Those Striker boys were raising every kind of hell at the time they pounced on you. You were by no means the only girl they violated, though it appears you were the only one who — " Breaking off, he shook his head. "What became of the child?"

"It died at birth," Grace Tucker answered. "I delivered it alone — in the ignorance of my eighteen years. Perhaps that was why the boy died. Though — though I'm glad he did. These parts can do without another male sprung from that seed." Covering her eyes with her hands, she shuddered. "My God! What a dreadful thought."

"Wish I could say something that would help," Gunn said regretfully. "But there's nothing that even starts to help a case like yours."

The tall blonde lowered her hands again, and visibly pulled herself together. "You don't have to feel sorry. I've lived with it long enough. It's history now,

Jed. But folk still hold it against me. Once in a while I go into town — to sell pelts or buy lamp oil — but the contempt is still in their eyes and voices."

"You're an outcast, Grace," Gunn remarked, glancing round the interior of the log-built cabin as uncritically as he could and noting that, along with the crude furnishings which he had already recorded mentally, her home possessed no more than the bare essentials of life for one person — a pot for cooking, another for coffee, a linen chest on the left of the hearth and a wooden armchair on the right, a fishing pole lodged above the window, an axe suspended from nails beneath it, a Winchester rifle propped in the vicinity of the tool, and a suit of buckskins and a coonskin hat hung at the back of the door. "You, the daughter of an Army surgeon, and raised a lady. It seems terribly wrong, Grace, yet I have to be glad of your misfortunes. If it hadn't been for them, I'd be dead."

"It's a way of looking at it," she admitted.

"How did you come to be out there tonight?"

"A fox has been killing my chickens," she replied. "I was out to kill the fox."

"Let's hope the fox hasn't got another of your birds while you've been worrying over me."

"He probably has," Grace Tucker said wryly, her face expressive of loneliness and small concerns. I caught your horse. At least, I imagine it's yours. It was loose on the Yellowstone Trail. I've tied it up outside."

"I expect it's mine," Gunn said. "I got swept clean out of my saddle. Those Striker brothers had a rope strung across the trail. What was I doing in these parts?" He explained how he had come to hear that his father was ill and ridden down from Laurel to visit him. "In fact I found him dead," he concluded, "and was on my way back to Montana when the Strikers caught me."

"Still that old trouble between you and them?" Grace asked shrewdly.

"Yes," he admitted. "In that respect, Grace, your life and mine are a little alike."

"But how did they know where and at what time you'd be travelling?"

"A bit more of the past," he said, and went on to tell her of his youthful love affair with Marissa Coates, Marissa's unforgiving attitude today, the fact that she was Alec Striker's current lady love, and of the betrayal which was the only possible explanation of how the Strikers had learned of his presence in Wyoming and known where to lie in wait for him.

"It's quite a terrible story," Grace Tucker said indignantly. "How could she have done such a thing? She must have been fully aware that it could mean your death. Why, she prompted murder, Jed!"

"She set me up," he acknowledged grimly.

"So she's Alec Striker's sweetheart,"

the blonde mused. "We find our own, don't we just. She never loved you, Jed. What pride of self she must have!"

"We must all have some pride," Gunn commented. "But you're right — hers is the wrong sort."

"Are you still going back to Montana?" Grace asked.

Gunn was about to answer in the affirmative, but then he hesitated. His mind and body had received real punishment, yet out of it was emerging a new iron. No longer was he quite so bent on the quiet life and the passive way. He felt ready to face extreme effort and the ultimate risk. There was something here that could not be left to run a cowardly course. He would flee from the Strikers no longer. They had pushed their wickedness too far. He was going after them. He knew it now — willed it even. It was just a matter of deciding how best to begin. "No, Grace," he heard himself say. "I'm not going back to Montana — yet anyhow."

"You're going to settle your account with the Strikers," the blonde said. "I can see it in your face."

"You see pretty good."

"Perhaps because I see what I want to see."

"You proposing a partnership of revenge?"

"You'll need an ally — all the help you can get."

"This is not a thing to be lightly undertaken," he agreed. "There are guns I can call on — friends in my need — but I'm not sure about that."

"The men of the Link B-G?"

"Yes."

"Well, there you are!"

"It's a matter of obligation, Grace," he retorted.

"They want me to take over where my father left off. I don't want to run the ranch; I want to sell it."

"That's your decision, of course."

"You don't approve?"

"Jed, it would be presumptuous of

me to say anything either way," she observed.

"But I want you to, hang it!" he snorted.

"Is it that you don't really know what you want?"

"Not beyond this," he admitted. "Not anymore."

"You were a wanderer, Jed — a loner with a fiddlefoot."

"I love the summer breeze and the smell of the tall trees, Grace. I always will. I hear the call of wild places."

"But a man grows older, Mr Gunn, and he simply can't ignore the responsibilities to which he was born."

"I know," he sighed, feeling that this conversation was remarkably intimate for one between two almost total strangers and remembering his earlier fear of the possible change he had sensed from atmospheres recalled. "Anyway, you're on, Grace. We must wait and see how it goes before extending it beyond the two of us. I'm not sure of where to start. I have a kind of half idea.

I'd like to go back to where it started for me. As I consider it for myself, it seems important, but I'm not sure that it would prove of much help to our joint purpose. There may be something of value to know, or just something to know. On the other hand, it could turn out there's nothing at all."

"You make it sound very mysterious," Grace Tucker said.

"Not really," he responded, thinking of Eagle Valley and what he suspected could be there. "I'd like to sleep on it."

"Then sleep on it," she advised. "You're lying on a bed."

"This is your bed."

"You need it more than I do," she said. "A blanket on the hearth will suit me very well."

"G'damn it no!" he snorted. "I wouldn't sleep a wink with you lying rough. If it's my horse outside, there's a first class blanket-roll tied to the cantle pins, and I'll be happy to bed down on the hearth."

"As you like," she returned. "I'm not holding an argument with my partner over a thing like that. My one concern is to see the Strikers laid low. If I can see that, I'll be happy to pay with my life."

"Don't get too prodigal," Gunn warned.

"This is the one thing I've dreamed of," she said — "the one opportunity I've prayed for. My life goes nowhere, Jed. I have no future."

"You've got as much as you want to have," Gunn said, grunting as he turned his feet to the floor and very slowly straightened up. "You've proved you're not a quitter. You're a fine woman, Grace; a man would have to go many a mile to see a finer. You've come this far, and you'll go the rest of the way."

"You're hurt, Jed," she observed anxiously, seeming to ignore his attempt to comfort.

"Some of Alec Striker," he agreed. "The varmint kicked me where a man can't stand a lot of kicking."

"Let me fetch your blankets."

"No — no," Gunn hurried firmly. "Must do it myself. Must keep moving. It's fatal to let a hurt freeze."

"It's dark outside, and you won't know where you are. I'll take you to where your horse is."

"If you think it necessary, Grace."

She went to the door and opened it. Damp air came in, swirling. She stepped outside, and he moved towards the exit — his steps short and tight — and he had to make a conscious effort to lift his left foot the necessary two inches to take it across the threshold. He saw Grace Tucker waiting for him where the lamplight ended on the wet earth before the hut. She turned, beckoning, and led him to the left, and he followed her beneath a tree and up to a hitching post which he judged to stand at the back of a small clearing in the woods that he could hear stirring around him. A horse drooped at the post and, passing a hand over the conformation of the brute's head and shoulders, Gunn knew

66

it at once for his own. "Yes, it's mine," he said, moving to the cantle and there untying the blanket-roll from behind his saddle. "Thanks, Grace."

"You're welcome, Jed."

Lifting down his blanket-roll, he tucked it under his right arm and said: "Let's get back indoors. There's a nip in the air."

Grace faced about and began leading the return, but they both checked abruptly as a succession of shots boomed across the land from somewhere to the south of the moon that was just visible through the branches ahead. The echoes went grumbling round the hills, and a coyote raised its plaint. "What was that?" the blonde asked tensely.

"Could have been men shooting at each other," Gunn observed. "I'm not so interested in the what as where."

"Isn't your ranch over that way?"

"It is," he acknowledged. "Those shots could have been fired on the Link B-G. But then there's a lot of country over there, and echoes do confuse. It won't do much good to worry over something we're not sure about. No doubt we shall find out in due course if it's anything that need concern us."

They resumed walking, and re-entered the cabin a few moments later, the girl putting the bar on the door behind them; and then she went to her bed and sat down upon it, while Gunn unrolled his blankets on the hearth and removed his gunbelt, only now conscious, oddly enough, that he had either lost his Colt when he had fallen from his horse or had it taken from him by one of the Striker boys without being aware of it. In practical terms, the loss of the revolver was a serious one — since a handgun was the weapon for emergencies — but he had a Winchester booted on his horse and would not have to walk unarmed; so he cast the belt over the back of the wooden armchair and forgot his loss. Then he lay down fully clothed, pulling a blanket over himself as Grace Tucker blew out the lamp and got into bed, and after that the red inconstancy of the flames in the fireplace broke and tossed the blackness that filled most of the cabin, highlighting the strangest fragments of the room for split seconds at a time.

Gunn closed his eyes, willing sleep, but he was more uneasy about the recent sounds of firing than he had cared to admit and failed to drop off immediately. With the Strikers roving the night and cock-a-hoop over what they must still believe to be his death, there was the chance that they had paid the Link B-G ranch house a visit with some form of disruption in mind that he could not even presently guess at; but he realized that his imaginings were speculative in the worst sense of the word and gradually forced them out of his mind, falling into a sleep now that was almost as deep as the unconsciousness from which he had lately emerged thanks only to Grace Tucker's efforts.

He awoke to find the cabin full

of grey morning light. Rolling onto his back with an effort, he yawned cavernously, his body feeling sluggish and his wits thick. Indeed he felt so far below normal that he doubted he would last the day out and, left to his own desires, he might have gone on lying there indefinitely; but the smell of coffee and the sight of legs stepping over him as a female shape bent towards the fire reminded him that he was Grace Tucker's guest and had last night projected a busy day for them. "Good morning," he rubbered out. "Guess I'm in the way."

"Somewhat," the blonde agreed. "Coffee?"

He saw that she was offering him a tin mug filled with the beverage. Raising himself on his left elbow, he took the hot drink and began to sip, his rope-burned throat almost closing up in its refusal to swallow the liquid at first.

"Okay?" she asked anxiously.

"I reckon," he replied, noting now

that she was clad in her suit of buckskins. "Ready for work, eh?"

"In your time, Jed," she answered matter-of-factly. "You wanted to sleep on something last night."

"So I did," he said. "And do you know what? I'd like to sleep on it again. But that won't do, will it? We've got to start somewhere, and our actions must serve an end — otherwise we're going to finish up nowhere.

"Grace, we were a mite hot-tongued in our talk last night, and I feel we've got to be more moderate in what we think and say this morning. You hate the Strikers — and so do I — but we're not bent on murder. If laying up with a rifle had been your style, you'd have done it long ago.

"No, while I'm sure we're both prepared to kill if we have to, we must also keep our doings within bounds, and try to arrange events so that we can call on the Federal law when we feel that the right moment has arrived. Therefore, we need to get

71

something big on the Strikers that, once named, will bring in a riding marshal without delay.

"Here's how I see it — " He went on to give an account of what had happened on the day that the late Mort Weir had crossed his trail, telling how his inquisitiveness had made the Strikers his enemies, and ending: "I have a sort of vague suspicion the Strikers could be guarding some kind of haven for outlaws in Eagle Valley. Like the Hole in the Wall or Robber's Roost. Those boys own hundreds of acres of prime grass, but they run few cows upon it, and they don't appear to have been too active as crooks in recent years. Yet, from what I've gleaned, they live the life of Riley. That requires money — a lot of it. Where, then, are they getting it? Ma and Pappy Striker didn't leave them much but the family poison, I can tell you that."

"It's an interesting question," Grace Tucker admitted. "Yes, they could be drawing money from crooks they're hiding. I think it's worth looking into anyway."

"I'm glad you think so," Gunn said. "I wish it wasn't such a long and exposed ride round to the eastern end of Eagle Valley. It will mean stealing across miles of Striker land, and then taking the biggest risk of all when passing into the valley through that crack in the cliff." He studied the thoughtful expression on his companion's face. "You haven't got a horse, have you?"

She shook her head.

"That may be just as well," he observed. "It's a job better done by a man alone."

"That may not be necessary," Grace Tucker responded. "I've been told of a way into Eagle Valley from the end nearest to us. I've never been through it myself, but I've been assured that it's there. And my source has yet to get anything wrong."

"Your source?"

"His name is Roaring Bear. He's a

Blackfoot chief, and I'm proud to call him my friend."

"What does he call you?"

"White daughter sometimes, but Hunter-woman mostly. He's had seventy years of life, and he's a grand old gentleman."

"How'd he come to tell you that about Eagle Valley?"

"His tribe used once to use it as a short-cut to Bear Creek," the woman explained. "The beaver over that way are exceptionally good. What money I manage to make comes through trapping. Roaring Bear has often helped me to the best return on effort."

"We should all have such friends," Gunn said. "Though it's plain you've needed them more than most. Very well, Grace. We'll seek Roaring Bear's door into Eagle Valley; then, if it's there, see what we shall see."

4

THEY made a plain breakfast of rye bread, stockfish, and coffee, then left the cabin about three-quarters of an hour later. Gunn held the barrel of his inverted Winchester across his right shoulder, while Grace Tucker held her rifle under her right arm. They strode purposefully into the woods beyond the woman's home, moving eastwards in the direction of the grey cliffs that were occasionally visible through the treetops before them as a line of high and often jagged stone that followed an approximate line between north and south.

From time to time, they held further conversation on the main subject that had exercised their minds the previous night, and were now fully agreed on the more sensible attitude which he had suggested they take to their vengeance plans on awakening. Grace Tucker was still full of her willingness to give up her life in order to see the Striker boys laid low, but she did appear to have grasped that Gunn had a more practical attitude towards the matter than her own. He had made it plain that he saw a future beyond their grim undertaking, and had no time for fatalistic sacrifices or the kind of excesses that might take them to court on serious charges. He now regarded the elimination of the Strikers as a job of work to be carried out with whatever resource and efficiency were demanded, and he had completely turned his back on the incipient fanaticism which he had felt after Grace Tucker had revived him from near death. But, while he did not intend to step outside the law for any major reason that could not be justified, he did accept that events might force circumstances on him that would have to be countered by any means at all, and he had geared himself to deal with emergencies on their merits as and when they came.

They had walked about three miles when the trees ended and the rocklands that crossed the foot of the bluffs began. Still hurting in the throat and pelvis, Gunn realized that, though he had slogged it this far without showing strain, his normal levels of mobility had been considerably reduced, and the sight of those cliffs — rearing vertically in places and wickedly undermined and overhung in others — daunted him far more than he dared admit. While he felt sure that he could drag himself up a steepish slope, he was also certain that any form of serious climbing would prove beyond him, and he was afraid that he might feel compelled to decline the risk that his hurts would represent to both his companion and himself if the western entrance to Eagle Valley — which still had to be located — should prove to have approach slopes that were too physically demanding for him at present. But he reckoned he would put all that into words only when he must; and for now he simply asked: "Have you the first idea of where to start?"

Grace nodded, though there was a frown upon her face as she cast her eyes back and forth along the rimrock. "I was told to look for the buffalo's brow and the beard beneath it. I take the latter to be a scree-slope. It can't be far away. As he stood outside my cabin door, Roaring Bear spoke of the rising sun as a marker. Due east. We can't have strayed far from the cardinal point in the few miles we've walked."

"You're right there," Gunn agreed. "But the ground tilts a bit to the south, and we may have tended with it. Let's walk to our left for half a mile or so."

Turning, they began walking northwards, their eyes peering towards the rimrock, and they had not gone far, when a brownish and massively rounded coping in a section of the summit stone appeared above them. There could be no question that this feature resembled the brow of a bison, while beneath it fell a slope littered with talus that could easily be pictured as the beard to go with it: "I think that could be what we're looking for," the blonde said, pointing.

"I reckon it must be," Gunn muttered, gnawing at his lower lip. "But I'm jiggered if I see anything that looks like a way over the top."

"Does it have to be over?" Grace wondered. "It could be through."

"That looks even more unlikely," Gunn commented.

"Well, I'm going to climb up there," the woman informed him stoutly. "You please yourself what you do. If Roaring Bear says there's a way to the other side, that's good enough for me."

"Okay, okay," Gunn soothed, tongue in cheek. "I can see I shall have to walk humbly in the shadow of this Blackfoot chief." He lowered his rifle to the trail position. "I reckon you'll have to excuse me; I'm not quite myself today."

Grace Tucker gave him no further attention. Turning from him, she began to scramble upwards. Shrugging to himself, Gunn moved after her, climbing a yard or so to her right and, his face bending closer and closer to the slope as his efforts increased, tried to draw level with her, but she stayed out in front, moving with the light, free action of one superbly fit, and he soon found himself gritting his teeth and shaking off the sweat as the angle of the incline increased its steepness as he went higher and his bruises and greater weight hampered him. He felt the temptation to declare himself incapable of going on; but, though he deplored it in himself, something in the blonde's attitude had set off his pride and competitiveness, and he kept his left hand reaching and the muscles of his legs and hips working strongly. He failed to close the gap, but was still there when they entered the final stages of the climb and Grace suddenly checked in her movements and called: "Look! Do you see the daylight through the rimstone? There is a way!"

"You sound surprised," Gunn chipped. "I was the one with the doubts."

"Oh, come on!" she protested, digging in her toes and once more straining onwards and up.

Gunn had not stopped ascending, and he could by now quite easily see for himself the light that slotted through the rimrock. He could also make out the great wing of slate which had slipped from higher up and come to rest — perhaps many thousands of years ago — with its lower edge so masking the rift that the phenomenon was invisible from ground level. Indeed a climber had to reach a height of around four hundred feet before he received the first hint that the crack in the cliff-top was there.

Gathering himself for one more effort, Gunn went at the last thirty feet of ascent. This brief stretch was fairly demanding, and also steep enough to become a real test of nerve; but he was careful not to look back and down, and watched with a trace of resigned admiration as Grace Tucker made her final scramble and slid head foremost into the rift. After that he threw his rifle into the fissure and, seizing at spurs of stone that jutted on either side of him, took his own last steps upwards and propelled himself headfirst into the rift, sprawling forward and then writhing into a space which he now saw to be much less confining than it had appeared when first glimpsed.

For a minute or so Gunn and the girl lay side by side, recovering their breath. Then Grace got to her feet and, holding her rifle at an angle across her breast, crouched into the five feet of headroom available and crabbed through the rift, passing out of its back and taking a careful step downwards that left her body visible to the watching Gunn only from the waist upwards. He rose also; then, picking up his rifle, ducked towards the spot where his companion now stood, moving into the open air as Grace Tucker had done and stepping down at the back of the fissure to stand beside her on the upper stair of the terraced descent that gave access to the floor of the huge valley that went yawning eastwards in the direction of a scene that Gunn knew to lie somewhat to the northwest of Blackford and to hold those features of the local terrain which he had encountered when shadowing Mort Weir six years ago.

Just then Grace Tucker turned her face towards Gunn and, shivering visibly, said: "So this is what the Blackfeet describe as the lost valley of the eagles. I don't like the place. It gives me goose bumps."

"It's the silence," Gunn said analytically. "I was once at the Hole in the Wall. You get the same feeling there. The sound of scree rattling seems to echo endlessly, and even the voice of the wind goes blustering over the top."

"It's so big and — and it seems so empty," Grace commented, the baffled look on her face and the slight break in her voice suggesting that she had no words adequate to the thoughts that she wished to express.

Gunn nodded silently, his gaze studying the eroded walls which shrank at almost even distances apart down the eye-dimming miles. He took in the bays and promontories, the slopes and terraces, the countless changes of colour, and the hollowing bottom rock that flattened finally into fields of dust and stone, splashes of water, fragments of meadow, and wavering lines of what looked like yellow-green fire where the dead scene split into the sudden life of banked greasewood clumps of aspen and willow, and corners of scrub-pine. A low cloud, dragging through crowns of caprock, spread vapours somewhere down the way, and the sun fired thin rainbows into the mist, while a shadow momentarily touched the earth as an eagle plunged out of the higher morning and came to rest on a northern crag, its presence lost the instant that it settled. Altogether, the valley gaped like some primeval wound which had never healed and appeared uninfected by the microbe humanity; but then, giving the lie to this impression and creeping like a suppuration on its mottled floor, Gunn made out the shapes of man and beasts. Just the one man, so far as his eye could be sure, and two mules. They were walking perhaps a mile and a half away, and approaching — over what now seemed to focus as a well-used path — a small huddle of buildings that stood in the shelter of the low black walls that formed the back of a kind of basement that was situated under the huge bluffs that reared along the southern side of Eagle Valley.

Now Gunn's mind snapped back to matters more immediate and, pointing, he said: "Seems to me we stepped out here just right. I could have looked for minutes along the valley bottom and not spotted those buildings on the right if it hadn't been for seeing that man and his mules."

"He looks familiar," Grace Tucker murmured. "He's remarkably big and fat."

"It could be Zeb Striker," Gunn said. "I recall that great heap and his waddling legs from years ago."

"Yes, I'm fairly sure it is Zeb," the blonde remarked, her sudden bitterness hinting at a most intimate contact with that bulk that still revolted her memory. "What's he up to, Jed?"

"He's got mules," Gunn observed. "Figures he's packing supplies into this butt end of nowhere. Grace, I do believe there *is* an outlaw haven yonder."

"Well, let's go and make sure of it," the girl said decisively, starting to move down the terraces that sprawled their irregular descent of the valley's western end.

Gunn stepped after her, and once more he had to watch himself as he moved his feet. The matter of his weight was less important to him now than it had been during his recent climb, but he still had to manage the stiffness in his lower body with the greatest care, for the way to the foot of the descent was still steep enough to throw him into a killing spin if some momentary hang-up should cause him to lose his balance and pitched him forward. Refusing to hurry, he picked his path in the most sensible manner he could, and still arrived on the valley floor within a minute of Grace Tucker's arrival there.

Slanting now towards the middle ground, Gunn remarked that he could see no risk to travelling over the easiest and most open of the going for the moment; so they stuck to the centre of Eagle Valley and walked without any need for deviation towards the area well down the place in which the buildings stood. About fifteen minutes later, they came to the grass about a pooling spring and the first of the vegetation which had been visible from beneath the western rimrock.

After that they were forced to be more careful as to their route, and they used whatever features of the valley floor were available for cover. Soon they began angling southwards, moving through stony lows and around banks where rocks bulged, but presently a ridge of some length appeared in their path and forced them to climb into a position of greater vulnerability before scuttling to a clump of firbrush on their left and concealing themselves again beyond the most open part of the crest. Pausing here amidst the coarse growth, they assessed their position in relation to the cliffs of the south, and were able to spot the roofs of the buildings glimpsed earlier on somewhat to the east of them and perhaps two hundred and fifty yards away over fairly open ground.

There was a birch stand situated rather more than a hundred yards closer to the buildings than they were at present, and Gunn and his companion agreed on the pale trees as their next stopping point. Crouching, they made for the timber at the run, halting now with the structures fully exposed; then, peering between branches, Gunn studied a site that had been laid out in the form of a semi-arc, with the fullest part of the curve opposite them and just a trifle to the right. Sharing this bend were a barn and a shed, while to the left of these — and beyond a yard of sorts — part of a house of the ranch type was visible. Then, again on the left and at the easterly tip of the semi-circle, a structure could be seen that was roofed with galvanised iron and had a chimney thrusting above its further end. There could be little doubt that this was a blacksmith's shop. For the rest, a corral that contained about a dozen horses was in sight on the extreme left, while a pit that was partially ringed with bushes balanced out on the extreme right. Here two men were fishing the unseen waters, but they appeared more interested in their pipes and yarning than in what was happening to their rods and lines.

"I don't think we need worry about that pair catching sight of us," Gunn said in a low voice. "Can you see anybody else around who might spot us as we move in closer?"

"No," Grace answered tensely, after looking about her carefully.

"Then let's make for the nearer end of the barn," Gunn urged. "We should get a good view of the house itself from the front corner."

Nodding, the blonde slowly worked the lever of her rifle, lifting a cartridge into the barrel and, grunting his approval of the precaution, Gunn did the same. Then, moving in the same stooped manner as before, they crossed the remaining ground between them and the buildings and halted against the back wall of the barn. After that, with Gunn leading, they rounded the angle on their left and catfooted to the front corner of the building's eastern side, stopping there with Gunn's head slightly advanced and the girl resting a palm between his shoulder-blades.

Gunn's eyes now rested on the front of the dwelling across the yard before him. The windows opposite were large ones, and through them he could see that the ground floor of the house had been fitted out as a bar and gaming hall. The big room was occupied by a number of hardbitten men and painted women. They appeared to be doing little but talk and drink, yet it was clearly a gathering of the lawless and their harlots. The atmosphere indoors was obviously a relaxed one, and this made it easy to recognise some of the male faces as being from among those most often displayed on the current crop of Wanted posters throughout these parts. Gunn felt absolutely confirmed in his suspicions — sure now that the Striker brothers had for years been making a lucrative living out of hiding criminals in Eagle Valley. And in some sense their success could be understood; for, when compared with spots like the Roost and Brown's Hole, this hiding place for the Wanted plainly offered a level of security and comfort such as no other haven in the Northwest — or perhaps even the entire West — could possibly offer.

91

Making signs for Grace Tucker to change places with him, Gunn stepped to the left and retreated a pace, allowing the blonde to advance into the position that he had just relinquished, and she took a long peep of her own towards the house, craning in due course to whisper: "I've just seen Abraham Sharkey in there. He's the most wanted man in the territory. He killed two men down in Cheyenne. I heard talk of it when I was last in town."

"I reckon we could make a list of the names in there if we knocked our heads together," Gunn said. "Never before did I see such a desperate set of villains."

"It's luck!" the girl breathed. "We now know what's here, and it's something we can use all right. But there's no sense hanging around, is there? Can we do any more here?"

"Don't figure what," Gunn replied. "Let's return to your cabin. But — be careful!"

"Goes without saying, doesn't it?" Grace responded. "Or is there — ?"

He jerked his thumb to the right, for it seemed to him that he had heard a faint sound from that direction just a moment ago. "Did you hear it?"

"Hear what?"

"Perhaps nothing," he said shortly. "I'm uneasy about what became of the fat man and his mules. There's no sign of him or his beasts near the house, but they've got to be around somewhere."

Grace Tucker murmured noncommittally. They faced about and began retiring. But Gunn had barely stepped beyond the rear corner of the barn when he heard an aggrieved voice that was not unknown to him call: "Hey!"

Checking, Gunn glanced sharply to his left and saw Zeb Striker standing in the space between the further end of the barn and the shed adjacent to it. The fat man stood with arms akimbo, and the heads of the pair of mules were visible behind him, the suggestion being that the brutes had been unloaded into the building on the fat man's left. Now, his face paling as Gunn and he stared into

93

each other's eyes, Zeb cried: "It can't be you! You're g'damned dead!"

Gunn put on a hideous expression and lifted his left hand, waggling the fingers. Then he emitted a graveyard wail and faked a step in the fat man's direction. Zeb backed off his eyes popping and his hair literally standing on end; but he was not quite as gutless as he looked and reached for the pistol holstered on his right hip, making a commendably fast pull and snapping off a shot. He was a split second slow, however, for Gunn had already brought his Winchester into line and triggered, though the bullet went rather lower than he had intended and did no worse than hit Zeb Striker in the top of his left leg. Shrieking his pain, the huge man eschewed the principle of the brave exchange and promptly went lolloping back into the space between barn and shed, the mules braying and kicking up with such half-crazed vigour that getting in a second shot at their driver was out of the question; and, lowering his rifle and shouting for the girl to follow him, he legged it towards the birch trees behind which they had previously hidden themselves to spy on the house. Then, reaching the stand, he turned onto the ground behind it and now used the trees as a form of cover, his limping run taking him at speed in the direction of places where flight could be fully concealed.

Grace Tucker drew even with his right shoulder. She kept her face to the front and matched him pace for pace. There was shouting behind him, questions and answers flying back and forth; and then a revolver went off and lead rattled among the branches to the rear. But amidst the echoes and the babbling voices confusion threaded raggedly, and Gunn had the feeling that he and Grace would be well clear of the haven before the folk indoors — and even the two fishermen at the pit — could arrive at a clear picture of the threat to their security which the recent incident had represented.

Much would depend on how well the wounded Zeb could express himself. If he could get his words out swiftly and coherently and horses could be saddled in record time — Gunn calculated that the blonde and he could still be overtaken, or fired on effectively, before regaining the exit at the valley's western end, and he silently cursed the fact that he had shot low when he had had the chance to kill the fat man; for, with Zeb's special knowledge of events out of the reckoning, it was fairly sure that he and his companion would have been out of danger by now. As it was, there must be trouble and complications ahead, and Grace and he could hardly call the next move theirs.

Through the stony lows they went, and round the banks, then past the little springs again and down the valley's open centre, their eyes fixed ahead and their minds still concentrated by fear and the need to run as far as they could while the chance was still there and their energies remained up to it. Their feet hammered, little puffs of alkali dust went up here and there, and their gasping held traces of agony. The great wall at the valleys western end was much closer now, and Gunn estimated that two-thirds of the ground that he and Grace had had to cover was already behind them. His confidence mounted, and he began to believe that things had gone so badly wrong for Zeb Striker and company back at the haven that there would be no chase; but then a splutter of firing from the rear disabused him on this point, and he craned over his left shoulder and saw a number of riders halted atop the best of the higher ground behind them and aiming rifles in their direction; but the range was long — and would soon become extreme — and, though he heard one or two bullets fall into the carpets of detritus nearby, he felt sure that it would be more by bad luck than marksmanship if either the girl or he were hit; and he prayed that the men back there would persist in their stupidity and keep shooting while they ought to be galloping after the running pair; for every yard now counted more and more in the progress of the fugitives towards the western end of the valley and the leisurely attitude of the outlaws was providing the best help possible.

But then, as he glanced back again and saw the measured manner in which the horsemen had started leaving their vantage and following a drooping shoulder towards the flat going down Eagle Valley's centre, he suddenly grasped that their casualness was a matter of ignorance rather than stupidity. They could not know — since it was improbable that Zeb Striker knew either — of the valley's western exit and were doing as they did in the belief that they had the pair on foot ultimately trapped against the bluffs at the end of the place anyway. In that was their real mistake, and the error could still be the saving of Grace and himself.

They entered the valley's final stage.

A mere quarter of mile would do it. Gunn spoke a hoarse word of encouragement to the woman in the buckskins, but he realized as he uttered it that the word was meant as much for himself as for her. Hardly aware of his body any longer, he forced himself to the limit, and sweat splashed away from him at every impact of his soles. Once more he sent a glance shooting across his left shoulder. The riders had holstered their rifles for the moment and were now picking up speed, but they were more than half a mile behind and Gunn judged that he and the girl had just about time enough.

Bearing left now, they raced for the point at the base of the terraces ahead which had seen their arrival in the valley after their descent from the rimrock. But then a pistol boomed, and the more confined echoes told their own story. "They're coming up — fast!" Grace Tucker gasped.

"Just — run!" Gunn croaked in response. "We can — do it!"

Two more shots thudded. Then the two split and tore into a volley. Lead struck about the running pair, an odd bullet shrilled, and the reverberations pulsed dully. Gunn no longer dared look behind him. Some inward part of him reached beyond the limits of the flesh. It was simply a mad rush for the giant steps that led to the rimrock and the exit slot beneath it. One supreme effort followed another, but their progress seemed to be getting slower, and Gunn was almost sure that, through the wash of blood in his ears, he could now hear the rumble of pursuing hooves. He dashed at the salt stinging in his eyes. Keep going — keep going! Then wonderfully — incredibly — they were there.

Up the initial slope they went, scrambling; and then they sprang from one level to the next, clawing. They zigged and zagged — straining and occasionally slipping, but never pausing — and, as the guns closed in below and the bullets hammered ever nearer to their bodies, they drove on and upwards into a state of recklessness that would normally have spelled disaster, but somehow they survived both the lead and the forcing madness of mind and muscle, heaving at last onto the topmost step of their ascent; then, pursued by a final clamour of ricochets, they dived into the rift and literally rolled through it, sliding now into a heel-digging descent of the westward facing slope beyond which took them to the limit of the "beard" and on down the remainder of the acclivity, delivering them in a sweat-drenched, wild-eyed relief to the rocklands at its foot and a final staggering run into the woods beyond, where they sank to their knees in almost total exhaustion and let the worst of their body heat and tension dissipate in half a minute of immobility and silence.

After that, as by tacit agreement and breathing heavily still, they crawled round and looked up at the pale 'brow' shaped into the rimstone, and Grace asked: "Will they come through, Jed?"

"Doubt it," Gunn replied. "They can't know what's on this side — and they are all fugitives."

"Yes," she agreed after a moment's thought. "But that won't stop some new move from the Strikers."

"Right," Gunn agreed. "But, far as we can be sure, Zeb was the only one of the brothers in the valley. He's got a slug in his leg, and I don't think he's likely to rejoin the rest of them in that much of a hurry. We've got time, Grace. It's not all against us — now."

"So what do you plan to do next?" the blonde inquired.

"About the one thing I can," he answered grimly, for fate seemed to be forcing him down that road which he was still far from sure he wished to take. "I must go to the Link B-G and ask for the help of my father's crew. We may be able to catch Alec, Colin and Dan Striker at home, then ride on and put the stopper on whatever we find in Eagle Valley."

"It sounds almost too easy," Grace Tucker mused.

"Easy's the word," Gunn gritted, helping her to her feet and using the muzzle of his Winchester to point homewards. "Pray heaven it can be brought off as smoothly as I've figured."

Yes, it was once more a matter of faith — but he didn't have too much of that.

5

STILL very tired from their efforts, but thoughtful also, they arrived back at Grace Tucker's cabin about an hour later. The girl wanted to make coffee and provide Gunn with something to eat; but Gunn, still very sensitive to the time factor, did not feel able to give a second thought to bodily needs and went almost at once to the clearing in which his horse stood tethered and Grace kept her chickens cooped. Here he thrust his Winchester into its saddleholster; then, leading his mount to the blonde's door — where she stood waiting, with arms folded and a slightly anxious expression on her face — gave a smile and said: "I'll be going then."

"One moment, Jed," she urged. "Is it safe for me to stay here?"

"If there's somewhere else you can

go," he responded, "I'd go. There are still a hundred-and-one ways this could turn out; and, as I've little doubt the Strikers know where you live and such, it's always possible they could come this way with some kind of revengeful harm in mind."

"I know of some caves," she said, "and I feel tempted to hike to them. But it seems to me the action must take place elsewhere. How I wish I had a horse, then I could come with you!"

"I'm glad you haven't, and can't," Gunn said bluntly. "Men are going to die before this is all over, and you've been shot at enough for one day." He mounted up, settling with a forward tug at his stirrups. "I can't tell you what to do — but I've just told you what I think you'd be best advised to do."

"Will you come back some time?"

"When I can," he assured her. "If I don't find you here, I'll know you've taken out for the time being."

"Very well."

"Where are those caves?"

"West of here and north — towards Clark's Fork — in the cliffs behind an Indian burial ground."

"Got you," Gunn said, raising a hand and kneeing his mount forward. Then he turned right along the cabin's southern wall and headed westwards, ducking low branches and riding round trees when necessary, and presently he came to the Yellowstone Trail. Here he drew his mount's head to the left and picked up to a canter, passing the oak tree only a minute later where a severed rope hung down from the lowest bough jutting towards the trail and offered whatever reminder he needed that he was still much less than twenty-four hours beyond the closest brush with death that he was ever likely to have and live to tell of it.

Chilled by the sight, Gunn felt a depressive reaction setting in, and he deliberately put out of his mind all that had happened to him since he had come over from Montana yesterday and thought now only about what might lie ahead. He galloped his horse because it wanted to gallop and, with the day brightening about them, the animal rapidly covered the ground between them and the Link B-G.

They came to the northern edge of the Gunn pastures. By now the skies were blue behind patches of running cloud, and the peaks to west and east of him were rising hazily into a sunlight that contained a September warmth that belied yesterday's rain and chill airs. But, despite the increasingly clement atmosphere, Gunn felt no answering lift in his being and sensed something ominous in the scene about him, for though he saw cows in plenty ahead of him he could see no sign of men working them and, as this should be the time of the Fall round-up, there ought to be maximum activity everywhere. True, the Link B-G was a big ranch and the hands could be down back of the bench on which the home buildings stood, but it was unlikely that more than part of the crew would be there, for the herds preferred the graze that spread down to the creek on this eastern side of the ranch house and most of them were kept there.

Gunn picked up the ranch trail, as he had the night before — though by his own eye now rather than his mount's instinct — and he bent westwards across the range and approached the huge green terrace on which his home was perched. He kept his head turning, but still no trace of human life did he see, and the noise of those shots — heard last night while he was collecting his bed-roll from his saddle in the obscurity of the woods — kept coming back to him. Then, with an abruptness that he found startling, he dismissed his doubts and questioning and accepted as a matter of plain fact that something here was indeed badly wrong, and he drove in his spurs and crossed what remained of the lower grass at full gallop, racing up the eastern face of the bench after that and then following the cart track in the direction of the outbuildings that formed a curve towards the back of the height and over to his right.

He reined to a halt in front of the bunkhouse; then, springing out of his saddle, he tied his horse at the crew's hitching rail and glanced up at the cookhouse chimney. No smoke curled there, and the feeling of desertion now hung over the site like an almost tangible presence. Putting his best foot forward, Gunn strode round his mount's rump and made for the bunkhouse, opening the door and thrusting his head inside. "Anybody about?" he shouted.

There was no answer. He called again, and got the same result. Then, feeling that he must confirm the absence of all personnel, he bowed indoors and looked around the dormitory, noting that the floor had been swept, the bunks were made, and the windows cleaned. After that he stalked to his right and shoved open the door that connected the kitchen with the living quarters. Stepping into the cooking space, he turned a slow circle. This revealed that here again all the cleaning had been done, the pots and pans were in correct order on the shelves, and the provision bins had their lids squarely in place. Everything looked just right — which was all very well — but not quite what he would have expected; for the cook should have been at his stove, turning out bread and such as fast as he could, while his assistant should have been driving the chuck waggon around the ranch to get food to the hands working the round-up.

Brow furrowed, Gunn withdrew from the kitchen and then the bunkhouse; and, walking along the front of the building, he turned right and passed between its western end and the barn next to it, heading now for the rear of the bench. He covered the necessary hundred paces or so and came to the western edge of the terrace, where he stopped and gazed into the immediate distance, praying for some glimpse of a man among the cows, but there was no movement of the kind he sought anywhere; and he faced round and walked back in the direction from which he had come — hoping to think up some explanation of this abandonment that need not spell disaster — and he did wonder whether the crew could have broken off and formed an honour guard to escort their dead employer's body into town; but he could not really give that one much credence; for, while John Dingle, the foreman, might have such an idea, he most certainly would not denude the entire ranch of labour in the round-up season just to carry it out.

The mystery had to be solved, and Gunn decided that all he could do now was ride into Blackford. He might be able to find out, from one source or another there, what had happened at the Link B-G. Passing between barn and bunkhouse again, he had rejoined his horse, when he sensed a movement at the back of the ranch house and gazed across the fences of the nearby main corral to see that Gwen Coates had just emerged from the kitchen door and was staring rather fixedly in his direction. "Gwen!" he shouted. "Where the hell is everybody?"

The woman staggered visibly; then, reaching to her right, she grabbed the end of a nearby windowsill and hung there, her face ashen and seamed with strain. Fearing that she had been taken ill and was about to faint, Gunn went dashing towards her, bending his course round the sides of the corral, and she was still in a state of semi-collapse when he arrived at the back door and gave her the support of his two hands. "Bear up, old girl!" he urged. "What is it?"

"They told me," she whispered — "that you were dead."

"I should have thought of that," he said, giving her arms a fond squeeze and her body a little shake. "I guess the Strikers came here last night. That's what those shots I heard were about. What happened?"

"You gave me such a scare!" the woman gulped, pulling herself together.

112

"My mother swore to her dying day that she saw the ghost of my brother, a year after his death at Antietam and dressed as he was the day he went off to war. I always laughed at her, but just now I thought — "

"Yeah," Gunn drawled with grim humour. "A glimpse of my mug scared Zeb Striker more than somewhat; but that fat bastard — begging your pardon, ma'am — had it coming! I'm no ghost, and far from it as you can get. Those thrice accursed brothers left me hanging from that bough a mite too soon. Grace Tucker — remember her? — came out of the night and cut me down in the nick of time. She revived me. That is some woman!"

"I'm glad you can say that," Gwen Coates said emptily. "I don't know what my daughter is. I didn't feel able to go home after Alec Striker had told me how she betrayed you. Oh, Jed!" A terrible sob tore itself from her. "I'm so sorry, son!"

"Don't be," Gunn urged. "It was none

of your doing. Marissa has got to live with it."

"If you wanted to kill the little witch," her mother said brokenly, "I couldn't blame you."

"I don't want to kill her," Gunn said indifferently. "Fact is, Gwen, I can no longer look low enough to see her. Yet I'm sorry for her too. What happiness does she think she'll get of a man like Alec Striker?"

"They deserve each other, Jed."

"Don't they just!" Gunn agreed heartily. "So what did happen here last night? You haven't told me yet. Where are the hands?"

"You'd better come into the kitchen," the woman said. "I've got some coffee on."

"No time for that," he said, though he was no longer sure of what there was time for, what came next, or anything else about it; since, whatever the facts of last night turned out to be, it was obvious that the straightforward plan which he had outlined to Grace Tucker

114

had come unstuck in its most important particular — for instant help was no longer available here — and he could only raise his voice a trifle and insist: "Tell me, Gwen. You must."

The woman nodded. "The Striker brothers rode up to the house last night. It was after midnight, and they kicked their way indoors. They told me that they had lynched you and left your body hanging beside the Yellowstone Trail. Then they ordered me to wake up John Dingle and call him into the house. I obeyed — what else could I do? — and John dressed and came over here, wearing his revolver. Alec Striker then repeated what he had said about hanging you, and told John Dingle that he wanted all the Link B-G riders off the ranch by the breakfast hour today. As I understand it, he and his brothers intend to invoke the reversion clause in the Range Laws and take over the Gunn grass on the grounds that there is no longer an owner living.

"John argued it. He said that Alec

Striker was mad and could not do such a thing. But Alec insisted that he could — that the situation was a fairly common one — and that the courts have always allowed judgment in favour of the invoker when an heir cannot be found. Anyway, the wrangling went on — and I was terrified that it was going to turn violent — but I believed everything was going to be all right when Alec Striker announced that he had spoken his last word — his will must be done — and he was about to leave.

"They all went out the front together. Then the row flared up anew. I heard Dingle call Alec and his brothers 'a pack of dry land pirates' and a few things less choice. All at once the shooting happened, and silence followed. I waited in the parlour, listening, and heard the Strikers ride away. When they were about a minute gone, I ran outside, a lamp in my hand, and found Dingle lying beneath the parlour window. He had a gun in his hand, had been hit by two or three bullets, and was dead. There was nothing I could do for him."

"Oh, heck!" Gunn exclaimed, feeling sick at the stomach. "John always did fancy himself quick on the trigger. Sounds like the blamed fool pulled on Alec. He wouldn't have stood a chance!"

"That's how it appeared to have been," the woman said heavily.

"Go on, Gwen. There must be more."

"Yes," she agreed. "Ray Forbes, the segundo, joined me from the bunkhouse about then. He was more cut up than words can say when he saw what had happened to John. He wanted to hear all about it, so I told him everything — including what I believed then had been your fate."

"And the crew pulled out in obedience to Alec Striker's order," Gunn growled. "Well, I can't really blame them. Men need a reason for taking action that may risk their lives. I'm about the same kind of man they are, when you get down to brass tacks." He ground his teeth nevertheless. "Oh, confound it! If those guys had been here, we could likely have avenged Dingle in short order and cleared up a lot else that isn't common knowledge yet."

"Forbes and the others made it clear that they were leaving the Link B-G for good," Gwen Coates said, a significant note in her voice; "but they also told me that they would be riding no further than Blackford today. They took Dingle's body in with them, and they intend to stay around town until after the funeral. I imagine that will take place tomorrow."

"So they're all together still," Gunn remarked. "I'll ride into town and have a talk with them. I need their help. Maybe they'll give it me, if I talk to them right."

"You'll only receive their help, Jed, if in return you keep this ranch running," she warned.

"Seems that's how it will have to be," Gunn said, brow corrugating as he acknowledged his final capitulation to himself. "It's not the life I really hanker for, but I guess it's the life that will have to be. Will you stay on here, ma'am, and take care of the house for now?"

"I have a home of my own in town, Jed," the woman reminded him, "and I much prefer it there."

"Such times as you feel able then?"

"Such times as I feel the place needs a woman's hand," she agreed. "But once you get here full time, I have the idea you'll have a wife to take care of things before we can say 'snap'."

Gunn didn't discount the possibility. "What about pa's body. Is it still here?"

"No, Jed. Wally Allen appeared with his hearse just before breakfast and picked it up."

"Thank goodness for that," Gunn said, turning away. "So long for now, Gwen. See you presently, eh?"

"Farewell-you-well, son."

His long strides took him back to the hitching rail before the bunkhouse.

Untying his horse, he backed it from the rail and forked leather, plucking its head to the right and kicking for a run, and he passed off the ground at the rear of the ranch house and then moved down the track on the eastern side of the bench to the range below. After that he galloped to the left of the cardinal point and travelled towards the high ground which protected the eastern flank of the sunken places which carried the local section of the Yellowstone Trail beyond the northern boundary of the Link B-G ranch.

Passing under the southern end of the protective ridge, Gunn saw the Striker grass on his left and followed an old track to avoid trespassing upon it. Riding almost due east now, he went on for a few minutes longer and cut the Blackford trail. Here he turned left and headed northwards over the partially walled and undulating way which served the town from this direction. It was about half a mile beyond the town that he saw, through a gap in the paralleling rock on his left and low upon the land beyond, the home of the infamous brothers whom he hoped to destroy. Of itself, the sight meant nothing to him, but it set him thinking; and he asked himself what indolent scum like the Strikers could possibly want with the thousands of acres of sheer hard graft which the Link B-G represented. There was no chance that the brothers would ranch it for themselves — or employ others to fatten cattle there — so the answer had to be in the easy pickings that would come from rounding up and selling off the Gunn herds and then using the grass to enhance the girdle of range private to the Strikers down this more thickly populated side of the secret route to Eagle Valley. There was no denying that the Strikers were capable of thinking big at times, but the ends they served were always small ones, and it required no great intelligence to see through their schemes.

The town of Blackford stood on

a flat between pine-clad hills. As he approached the place from the slightly elevated land to its south, Gunn saw the afternoon light playing on its slate roofs and shining off the puddles along its few and rather mean streets. Drawing closer, he perceived that half-hearted attempts had been made in the recent past to give the main street a solid foundation; but, as his horse trod the start of the thoroughfare, he saw that the hoggin used had broken out of its packing and lost all pretence of stability. This had created a dangerous state of looseness among the big round flints for hoof and wheel alike, and out of respect for his mount's legs, Gunn decided to dismount and walk his horse towards the centre of town.

Halting the animal, he swung down; then, holding the brute near the mouth and picking his way with care, he began walking between buildings, most of his mind occupied with how best to locate the cowboys from his late father's ranch. He reckoned that he might learn more at the undertaker's shop than anywhere and, seeing the sign that marked it jutting on the left of the way, he angled towards it, hitching his horse at the nearest rail and then walking into the crepe-and-lily bedecked front office, where he was met by Wally Allen, the proprietor. Allen was an Englishman of six-feet five-inches, large of belly and full of fruity-voiced benevolence, a grey-maned, smiling colossus who, after remarking that it was many a day since he had last seen Jed Gunn, offered his condolences on the death of the 'pater' and followed up with the ultimate conclusion 'that we must all tread the same sad path that leads to glory'. "I expect you've come to see what we've made of dear old Bert," he added. "Jed, he looks a picture, if I do say so myself."

"Good man," Gunn approved. "I hope you've done the same for John Dingle?"

"He's coming along nicely," the undertaker responded, dry-washing his huge white hands. "If you would like to come through to our chapel of rest — "

Gunn gave his head a shake. "Perhaps later on. Time presses right now, Wally. There's much to do. Can you tell me where I can find the Link B-G crew?"

"Indeed I can," Allen boomed. "They've hired a large part of Barkworth Hotel. I think they're presently holding what, for want of a better term, I must describe as an extended wake."

"Obliged, Wally," Gunn said and, facing round, returned to the street, where he freed his horse and resumed walking the brute towards the middle of the town, his right eye taking in the tall chimneys and steep roofs of the Barkworth Hotel, the largest building in Blackford.

Nearing the hotel, he crossed the street, and was preparing to secure his mount again, when he sensed somebody watching him from a spot still some distance ahead and on the opposite sidewalk. Glancing up, he saw Marissa Coates standing about fifty yards away and staring at him intently. A good deal of time had now elapsed since Grace Tucker and he had escaped from Eagle Valley, and he had no means of knowing what had been communicated to whom in the background. He could not be sure whether by now Marissa knew him to be alive or still thought him to be dead; but, whatever the fact of that, she appeared completely self-possessed and made an attractive figure in her fancy bonnet and shawl, while the shopping basket on her right arm added a nice touch of everyday domesticity. The girl studied him a moment longer; then, with an agility that almost deceived the eye, side-stepped into an alley on her right and was gone.

Controlling a desire to spit, Gunn spun his hitch. Then, after glancing hesitantly towards the alley and making up his mind that there really was nothing to be gained by seeking to corner Marissa and telling her what he thought, he put the girl's reappearance in events from his thoughts and entered the hotel by its front door, going straight to the reception desk and asking the clerk on duty where he could find the party from the Link B-G ranch.

"Ground floor, sir," the lantern-jawed and swarthy clerk replied, a lank moustache almost dragging in an inkwell as he squinted up from his short-sighted crouch over a ledger. "I reckon they're all herded together right now in the dining-room."

"Which way?"

"Straight ahead, sir — on down the hall. Past the withdrawing room and the bars. Last door on your right, sir."

Gunn spoke a word of thanks. He walked on down the hall, passed the rooms mentioned, and came to the last door on the right. Here he knocked loudly enough to be heard.

The woodwork opened to him, and a lean, rough-shaven face that he didn't know appeared in the gap, a hard but honest eye questioning mistrustfully. "What d'you want?"

"I'm Jed Gunn."

"Yeah," the other said wickedly, "and I'm Abraham Lincoln. The devil's downstairs." A thumb hooked. "Go away!"

"I'm Jed Gunn, and I'm not dead," Gunn bit. "Plain enough for you?"

The cowboy at the door looked uncertain; and then he craned over his right shoulder and called: "Ray! We got a feller here who says he's Jed Gunn and he ain't dead. That'd make him old Bert's son, wouldn't it?"

"If he's *that* Jed Gunn," a voice from within the dining-room conceded. "Wouldn't rate it a common moniker, Mack, but there could be another one."

Gunn heard a pair of feet approaching on the other side of the entrance. Then the door opened wide and a big-eared, fresh complexioned face that was faintly dusted with freckles and topped by fine ginger hair appeared above the harder and rather older one which belonged to the man who had answered the door to Gunn.

"I am *that* Gunn," Gunn insisted,

"and we don't know each other. You'll be Ray Forbes, the segundo."

"That's me," Forbes agreed, "and it's a sure moral you and I never met before, sir. But talk's cheap as hell." It was the segundo's turn to crane. "Hey, Wilkins! You were at the Link B-G in Jed Gunn's time. Come here and have a look at this guy. Tell us if he is the man."

More footfalls approached the doorway, and a third face, wide-jawed, narrow-browed, sad-eyed and grey down the sideboards, thrust into the space between jamb and woodwork, a slow grin lighting the sombre orbs a trifle. "Hi, Jed. Yeah, that's him, Ray. And he sure as hell ain't dead."

"Hi, Charlie," Jed responded. "Long time no see."

You'd better come in, Mr Gunn," Ray Forbes said, pushing his companions aside and stepping back himself.

Gunn entered the long and rather narrow room beyond the threshold, the highly polished refectory table at the centre of the floor picking up his shadow as did the big English sideboards standing against the walls on either side of the place. About the room something like a dozen and a half men were seated or lounging, some smoking cigarettes or pipes and others contemplating glasses of whisky or beer. "Gents," Gunn acknowledged, nodding around him in the friendliest manner that he could manage.

The movement of his head found a general response, but the grunts that accompanied the nodding expressed a lot of uncertainty.

"Your father's crew," Forbes introduced meaningfully. "These men gave Bert Gunn good service. We understood — "

"I know what you understood," Gunn interrupted. "I've heard about what happened to John Dingle too. I've just come from the ranch, and a talk with Mrs Coates."

"It's our plan to bury John," Forbes said, "and then break up and go our various ways."

"You don't have to pile the agony on, Ray," Gunn advised. "Mrs Coates told me. I need your help."

"You sure need something," Forbes allowed. "That's an ugly set of bruises you got on your throat."

"The Strikers hung me up — and made a good job of it — but a lady came along and cut me down just before the life left my body."

"It's happened before," the segundo observed. "A number of times. Now you want your revenge, sir."

"We can do without the sirs and the misters," Gunn said. "I'm plain Jed in this company. Yes, I want my revenge. But there is quite a lot more to it than nailing four hides to the barn door just to please me."

"Like the Link B-G, perhaps?"

"Like the Link B-G," Gunn admitted. "And then much else. I've discovered that the brothers Striker run a haven for outlaws in Eagle Valley. I need a body of guys like you to help me clean up."

"Eagle Valley?" Forbes queried. "From

what I've heard, the place is just there. Folk have in the past climbed into it, but there's no way into it at ground level."

"You, like most folk," Gunn returned, "have been misinformed, Ray. There are two ways into Eagle Valley without ropes and climbing gear. One is placed under the rimrock to the west, and the other is at ground level to the east. But neither approach is easy." He gazed around him, conscious of the lack of force and appeal in both his case and situation, and he prayed that the spirit of men present would make up what was lacking. "I have to ask it. Are you fellows with me? I know it's all kind of sudden and unexpected, but that's how things come up. I hope it goes without saying — and sounds like no part of a bribe, since you guys are free as the wind — that your jobs on the Link B-G will be there if we come through all right. I aim to run the ranch as it was run in the past. Looking at it now, I guess I should never have spoken otherwise to John Dingle; but, there we are, it's no good making excuses. All of us here are much the same breed of man, I reckon, and if you understand yourselves you like as not understand me."

"She's a caution!" Forbes commented, squashing his nose in a hard rub with the palm of his hand and snuffling. "Well, boys, you've heard the man. What's it to be?"

"Aw," Charlie Wilkins said inconsequentially, "I'd rather work for a Gunn than most. This here'll make something to do. I'm nigh crazed of sittin' around in this fancy pen and twiddling my thumbs."

"I second that!" a big man in the top right-hand corner of the room snorted sleepily.

"I third it," somebody else announced. "Me, I can't get out o' this doggone monkey house soon enough. I'll get provoked into shootin' the buttons off them snooty waiters if they treat me like a cowpat much longer!"

The mood had now been set, and a big chorus of agreement sealed the business.

"Sounds unanimous," Forbes remarked. "I don't figure we need take a vote on it anyhow. Okay, Jed — we're in. Tell us what you want."

Gunn nodded, and was sorting out that aspect of his thoughts, when a sudden rush of shadowy movements at the windows of the dining-room — which were two in the wall on the right and one at the foot of the chamber — caused him to switch his mind utterly and shout: "On your bellies — all of you!"

And no sooner had he suited his own action to the command than pistols blazed from without and glass flew, bullets lacing the room as the men looking in took full advantage of the surprise which they had created and simply pumped lead among the ranch hands.

6

A BULLET drove into the floor beside Gunn's left temple, and another angled across his back and whipped the skirt of his coat. Perceiving how vulnerable he was to the revolvers firing in through the shattered window at the bottom of the room Gunn raised himself on his hands and then drew up his knees, propelling himself into a shallow dive to his right and coming to rest behind a large and heavily carved dining chair which a previously seated cowboy had just vacated.

Slugs pursued him. They whacked and splintered the woodwork before him; and, realizing how little cover the chair was really providing, he reached for his empty holster in an overpowering desire to retaliate; then, cursing aloud in the impotence of his action he sent desperate eyes about him and felt a fleeting relief as he saw that one of the Link B-G cowboys had fallen a short distance to his left and dropped his pistol on the way to the floor.

The Colt rested less than a yard away on the varnished blocks that made up the level base of the room. Gunn reached for the weapon, and splinters stung his hand as lead ploughed across the cubes of timber. Ignoring the pain, Gunn thrust the index finger of his left hand through the pistol's trigger-guard and drew the Colt quickly to him, hooking it into the full grasp of his digits and then transferring it to his waiting right hand. Cocking the weapon, Gunn slid his chair to the left and once more brought himself opposite the window at the lower end of the room, seeing a man who stood four square to the frame, and he fired off an extended arm, aiming to kill, and his target buckled to the ground and was instantly replaced by a fleshy, rotten-toothed varmint whose eyes blazed out of piggy hollows that were bridged by shaggy brows. The newcomer triggered three shots at Gunn that ground into a continuous roar, and Gunn ought to have died there and then, for two of the slugs missed his head only fractionally and his brow was shielded from the third by one of the chair's oaken members that deflected it. This failure on the other's part gave Gunn the chance to take aim again and inflict another casualty on the killers outside the hotel.

There was now a good deal of confused movement and blasting within the dining-room, and the muzzles at the windows continued to flash and bang, helping to fill the place with a blackish-blue haze. Gunn looked for somebody else with whom to exchange fire; but, now that the shooting had become in some degree a two-way traffic, the men outside were far less willing to show the whole of their bodies in the window spaces than they had been half a minute ago.

Then, offering help to paralysed wits and men tied down by the incoming fire, Ray Forbes shouted: "The door's wide open, men! Crawl backwards and out into the hall! You'll no longer make targets through here!"

Gunn could see the truth of that. He wasn't far from the door and, leaving what protection his chair gave, he began crawling to the rear — as if leaving the presence of some mighty potentate — and, though several bullets skipped past him on either hand and he came into brief collision with another man who was moving in a similar purblind manner to himself, he soon found himself out in the hall and was able to break to the right and shove himself erect in the safety of the space near the building's rear. Forbes and several other men were standing close by, pistols in hand, and he joined in their anxious watch as more of the ranch hands who had survived the raking of the dining-room completed their slithering withdrawals from the smoke-filled chamber and clambered to their feet in the areas of safety on either side of its entrance.

Sensing the inertia and shocked fascination which held the onlookers, Gunn realized that they were all still in danger and also letting what could be an opportunity slip. He and his companions had not yet lost their chance to run outside and tackle the killers there while they were still spread along at least two sides of the Barkworth Hotel. The advantage of this situation could hardly be enormous, but it was a little easier to deal with enemies who were slightly split up rather than in a compact body, and there was the probability that he and his companions would be able to inflict serious casualties among the killers before they could group up again and then defend themselves with a collective fire.

"Let's go outside, Ray!" Gunn urged. "They won't be expecting us to take the fight to them!"

Aware from the segundo's expression

that Forbes had grasped the full import of his words, Gunn did not wait to discover whether he would be followed or not, but turned to the back door and wrenched it open. He found himself at once face to face with a scrawny-necked, wall-eyed villain, dirty of skin and greasy of hair, who brandished a pistol in the air while starting back from him in surprise. Gunn shot the fellow through the heart, then jumped over the sprawling body, snapping a shot to his left as a pair of badmen advancing there fired on him together, each missing him only narrowly.

Gunn realized in the same instant that he had missed too, and he re-cocked his weapon as fast as he could, but three or four other ranch hands had joined him in the hotel's back yard by now and discharged their Colts at the two badmen who had just blasted at him. The pair, confronted now by angry and vengeful odds which they didn't like, sprang round and pelted for the hotel's northern end, obviously intending to turn there and regain the main street, but bullets took the feet from under them before they could reach the corner of the building ahead, and they went sprawling on their faces and lay inert.

Keeping a few yards clear of the brickwork, Gunn dashed for the angle himself and arrived at the widest view of the ground towards the street that he could obtain. He saw a group of figures — among whom Alec and Colin Striker were prominent — in the act of turning off the sidewalk and heading for the yard at the rear of the Barkworth. Colin presenting the better target, Gunn triggered at the man. The other dropped his revolver and buckled to his knees, both hands pressed to his chest. Shifting his aim to Alec, Gunn squeezed off again, but this time his hammer fell on a fired cartridge and it was plain that the six-shooter which he had picked up from the floor was empty; but again Forbes and some of the Link B-G riders had taken up his case and the men nearer to the street had halted amidst a hail of fire.

Gunn stepped back into the cover of the corner brickwork. Examining the Colt in his hand, he was relieved to find that it was the forty-four calibre model which the ammunition in his gunbelt would fit — and, breaking open the loading gate, he pointed the muzzle of the weapon skywards and spun the cylinder, sending the spent shells from its chambers rattling to the cobbles under his feet. Then he prised new bullets from the loops of his gun-rig and re-charged the Colt in all six chambers; and after that he pushed the loading gate back into place and thumbed the hammer to full cock, running now to the street, where Ray Forbes and the Link B-G cowboys were stopped on the sidewalk and shooting steadily at the backs of the killers, who were presently in full retreat, Alec Striker and another man supporting the wounded Colin between them.

Gunn looked beyond the ground

which the withdrawing badmen had so far reached. He saw a dozen or more horses tethered at the rails on the opposite side of the main and towards the northern end of town. The mounts could only belong to the killers, and this was proved when, moments later, the first two or three of the surviving badmen reached the line of animals and freed their own horses, backing them to the centre of the street and swinging up.

The fugitives put steel to hide and away they went. Gunn turned his attention to Alec Striker and the man who was helping Alec with the wounded Colin. The trio were still not that far off and there was a lot of lead flying about them. They had been lucky so far, but he did not believe their luck could last, and he had no sooner had the thought than the badman assisting Alec with the injured Colin fell to the ground and took the crumpled Striker with him.

The curse that Alec vented in that

moment was dreadful to hear. He turned and fanned his revolver towards the Barkworth until it was empty. Then he thrust the weapon into its holster and bent over the fallen men beside him, shoving the dead or wounded helper uncaringly aside and lifting the motionless Colin by the collar of his shirt. One eye on Gunn and company, he peered into his brother's face; then, cursing again, he let Colin drop into the prone position and went for the tethered horses up street of him at a breakneck run, freeing the animal that presumably belonged to him and bounding into its saddle. Then, heels kicking and reins lashing, he sped away — chased fruitlessly by a final volley from the Link B-G cowboys — and within seconds had cleared the town's northern limits and was heading into the country, safe for now.

"We've got to get after them!" Gunn shouted in Ray Forbes's ear. "Where are you and the boys keeping your horses?"

"At Carlow's horse barn," came the reply.

"Fetch 'em — pronto!"

"Betcha," Forbes acknowledged. "But what about the guys lying in the hotel dining-room?"

"We must leave them to the attention of others," Gunn answered crisply. "What matters for now is to catch up with Alec Striker and those other sidewinders!"

Forbes said nothing more. Signalling to the men clustered around him, he made off up the street, heading for the tall wooden building on the left of the way which carried a board above the front door on which had been painted the legend: CARLOW'S LIVERY.

Gunn watched the running segundo and other men until they disappeared into Carlow's barn. He had counted them at the number of fourteen, which meant that something like half a dozen of the crew had fallen during the attempted dining-room massacre. It was bad enough, of course, but could have been much worse, and Gunn turned left and strode to where his horse stood in front of the Barkworth Hotel, sure that Alec Striker must be feeling right now that this was not his lucky day.

Mounting up, Gunn rode along the street to where Colin Striker and the other man who had been recently shot were still lying motionless. Several townspeople who had taken shelter indoors during the firing had just emerged again and were closing on the pair, but Gunn got to them first and dismounted again, kneeling between them and making such examination as was necessary. Both men were obviously dead. Colin Striker had a bloody hole just to the left of his heart, and he had been booked from the moment that the slug had pierced him, while the other man — the notorious Abraham Sharkey, Gunn suspected — had been shot through the skull and must have died instantly.

Stepping back, Gunn remounted, leaving the bodies to the care of the others; and, twisting in his saddle, he watched the ground in front of the livery barn for the reappearance of Ray Forbes and the Link B-G cowboys. As he sat there, he felt a trifle shamed by the glad feeling that he had at Colin Striker's death; but Colin had been second only to Alec in vileness and would be better under the ground. Indeed, to be honest, he felt no sympathy for any one of the seven badmen whom he knew to have fallen. They were undoubtedly scum from the haven in Eagle Valley — where the horses that he had seen had suggested the presence of around a dozen outlaws — and the attempt to kill off Gunn and the Link B-G crew had been about as dastardly and callous as anything that could be imagined. If anybody ought to have qualms of conscience, it should be Marissa Coates, for there could be no question that it had been her tip-off — after seeing him, Gunn, stop outside the Barkworth Hotel — which had enabled Alec Striker and his outlaw buddies to hit the ranchmen, whom Striker would have perceived as about to become his serious enemies under Gunn's leadership. Obviously, too, Marissa had been aware that Jed was still alive when she had seen him, and it was even possible that — after much rapid toing and froing in the background — she had been primed in her own home and playing the deliberate spy in expectation of Gunn's appearance in town. There was much here that he could only speculate on — and might never be sure about — but it could now be said Marissa's treacherous ways had been responsible for the deaths or woundings of thirteen or fourteen men, and folk who went on at that rate were not as a rule allowed to go on for very long. The girl was going to come to a bad end if she didn't watch out and, had it not been for the fact that he liked and respected her mother, Gunn would not have given a damn.

Ray Forbes and the Link B-G riders emerged from the livery barn about then. Going ahead, Gunn waved for the cowboys to follow. They rode out of town at a careful pace, and then went to full gallop. For the next half an hour they stayed at or about the maximum but, despite the rising nature of the terrain ahead, failed to bring Alec Striker and his party into view for even a single moment. Recognising that there was nothing to be gained in the circumstances by pushing the horses into a state of exhaustion, Gunn finally shouted for everybody present to slow right down and rest the steaming mounts at a gentle trot.

"Looks to me," Forbes observed, now riding at Gunn's right shoulder, "as if that bunch could be heading for the side trail which connects up with the Yellowstone Trail just short of the Montana line."

"My thought too," Gunn acknowledged.

"Alec Striker won't dare show his nose around Blackford again," the segundo commented. "Even Buck Lammas wouldn't allow that, and he's the most uncaring sheriff alive."

"You can say that again," Gunn agreed. "I'm surprised we didn't see something of him back in town."

"That's easy to explain," Forbes said derisively. "I heard it from Jake Carlow, while we were getting our horses. Lammas left town, riding south, about quarter of an hour before Striker and his lot started shooting us up in the Barkworth's dining-room."

"Did he now," Gunn mused. "You can think what you like about that."

"Yeah, so long as you don't think too loud," Forbes chuckled. "How far do you intend to take this chase, Jed?"

"Damned if I know," Gunn confessed. "We have no grub with us, and there's a ranch back yonder. I hoped we might do better on the chase than we have. Now here we are with a ride that could just drift on and finally splutter out."

"There *is* a ranch back there," Forbes emphasized — "and we've lost a third of the hands, including our foreman."

"As to that, you're the foreman now,

Ray," Gunn said. "If John Dingle was happy to have you as his under man, I figure you'll do for me."

"Well, thank you kindly, boss," Forbes said.

"We'll ride to the line," Gunn said with abrupt decision. "If we've seen nothing of Alec Striker and that outlaw bunch of his by then, we'll head back along the Yellowstone Trail to the ranch." He frowned at his own thoughts. "I suppose we've done some good, but I can't believe this is over. We'll just have to be patient and give whatever's to come time to develop."

Forbes nodded his acceptance of this, and Gunn and he became silent and watched the trail ahead. Behind them there was a certain amount of chit-chat among the riders, but the leading pair simply didn't know each other well enough to sustain small talk. Presently Gunn began to look about him, and now he let his concentration slip a trifle. He took in the huge, snow-crowned peaks of the Absaroka on his left and, at a greater distance on his right, those of the Bighorn range. Although the sun was still shining out of the now deep blue and almost cloudless sky, he felt the airy vastness of the north and a chill stealing around his ears out of far places where the frosts were forming again and the gales of the Fall were winding up. He loathed many aspects of the weeks and months that lay ahead — the piling whiteness, the freezing mists that hung above the iron earth, and the hanging waters which glittered under peaks that blew and streamed — but there could be no Spring without them; and he loved the Spring.

But where had he let his mind take him? No leader of men could allow himself to so forget his responsibilities. The side trail was now visible on his left and only fifty yards ahead. He could so easily have missed it in his reverie. Then what would the men have said? It seemed to him that everything had gone suddenly slack. If only there were a string that he could pull to bring it back into shape.

He signalled the turn. Now they clattered westwards over soil worn through to the underlying granite. From here it was five miles to the Yellowstone Trail. Soon they would be climbing and dipping on the rocky shoulders above sunken lakes, with the deepening light reflected at them off the pinewoods that marched up the steep slopes opposite the westering sun. It was just travel, exercise for the horses — and a chore.

They had begun ascending. Here outcropping stone edged the trail at numerous points. Reflecting that the underlay was too hard to give any indication that a body of horsemen had passed this way before them, Gunn found himself with incipient doubts about the change of direction that he had just made. For it occurred to him now that the badmen could have seen it more in their interest to follow the main trail into the wild and empty lands between the Yellowstone and the Missouri; and he was starting to wonder how far he could trust his own judgment, when a faint glint plucked at the corner of his left eye and drew his attention to the flattish rock levels adjacent. Sufficiently influenced, he reined in and, dropping off his saddle, walked across the outcrops to the spot about fifteen yards beyond the trail where the gleam originated, and he picked up what was obviously a recently cast horseshoe and lifted it under his eyes for a close inspection which revealed little of itself except for an uneven pattern of wear and the undoubted dilatoriness of a rider who must have had warning enough of the iron's state and ought to have had it replaced days ago. Indeed, had the shoe lain on the trail itself, Gunn would not have accorded it a second glance, but the fact that it had been shed so far off the beaten way could well invest it with a perhaps special significance.

Hearing the sound of a footfall

behind him, Gunn turned his head and saw Ray Forbes walking towards him from the nearby trail, where the Link B-G party had halted just beyond the place where his mount stood.

"What have you got there?" Forbes inquired.

Gunn showed the other the worn horseshoe. "Somebody could have thrown it over here out of the way," he admitted, as much to himself as the newly made foreman. "On the other hand, a horse could have cast it here just after leaving the trail."

"You suggesting Alec Striker and his bunch may have turned back on themselves?" Forbes asked.

"I guess that's the idea," Gunn said, looking across the granite levels before him to the grassy slopes beyond them that fell in a hollowed sweep from the stepped ridges that broke out of the high ground above the lower placed northbound trail which he and his companions had recently left. On the other side of the immediate fields of stone, about two miles away, he could see trees and also make out hints of broken country beyond. Thus, horsemen riding in that direction would, once they had put the nearby meadows behind them, move into sufficient cover to allow them to travel southwards without being sighted by riders cantering on the lower level and in the reverse direction. "Ray, the pointers are there all right. But why would they do it?"

"Alec could be heading back to his place to pick up brothers Dan and Zeb," Forbes suggested. "Were those two with him in town? Did you see anything of them?"

"No, I didn't," Gunn answered, not bothering to remark that Zeb had a leg wound and probably didn't feel too brisk anyway. "You're figuring blood is thicker than water. I wouldn't bank on that with a man like Alec. He'd hardly care about leaving Dan and Zeb behind. If that bunch *did* turn back, there was something more to it than that. Gain. Which equals robbery in their talk. Could be they hit on a sudden decision to do the unexpected. If Alec has fixed it so that he can no longer live in these parts, mightn't he want to empty the bank before departing for good?"

"Hey, that's a notion!" Forbes acknowledged. "Nobody in Blackford would be expecting a swoop on the bank after what's happened there today."

"It could work too," Gunn observed — "with the sheriff heaven knows where and us riding the wrong part of the ring. I reckon Alec must have had us under observation from up here some time recently."

"Back they come with their saddles loaded," Forbes mused, "and off they go in the direction of Miles City."

"Likely," Gunn agreed, throwing the worn horseshoe aside. "Let's return to our horses, then lead the party across yon field of granite. If we find sign on the grass at the other side, I reckon that we can take it our reasoning is about right. Okay?"

"Jake with me, boss."

Both men turned and hurried back to their horses.

7

RECOGNISING the risk to the legs of the horses on the treacherous surfaces of the granite outcrops, due care had to be taken in the crossing, and it took Gunn and his followers more than ten minutes to cross the relatively narrow danger area. Once off the rock levels, they began to quarter, and Ray Forbes called Gunn's attention to tracks in the still wet meadowland almost at once.

"Them all right," Gunn said confidently, studying the displaced divots and deep hoof impressions where the mounts of the party that had gone before had pranced a moment on the soft going and then launched into full gallop. "That sign has got hurry written all over it."

"They'll have to push it," Forbes remarked. "But give a look to our horses."

"Theirs can't be in better case," Gunn admitted. "And, short of getting a change of mounts — which I don't see how they're to manage — they'll have to nurse their horses more than we need to; so I don't figure they'll gallop for long. If we ride hard, there's a chance we can overtake them before they get to town and have our fight where innocent folk and property won't get harmed."

"Reckon we're all for that," the foreman said.

Gunn pointed to the front; then, using his rowels, set his horse reaching for the south. The other riders began pounding along in Gunn's wake. They traversed the acres that sagged across the middle of the high meadows, passed through the rear edge of the trees that came next, skirted a rockland, jumped a run-off, and arrived on another expanse of grass, eyes straining all the time for some glimpse of their quarry, but the miles slipped by without any sighting of Alec Striker and company on the skyline or land between.

Before long Gunn started eyeing the landmarks at the edges of the scene ahead. He estimated that he and his followers were now little more than four miles from town. He had expected to spot the badmen minutes ago — and again found himself wondering whether he had been out-thought — but these latest doubts concerning his leadership were not to be tested in the present circumstances, and he made up his mind that he and his party were going all the way to Blackford, regardless of the mistake that this might later turn out to be; but all at once he felt that he must modify his resolve; for, as the land ahead dropped into a low and then reared like a green wall, he glimpsed, on the black line formed where its upper edge cut the sky, the kind of small movement that could have been made as a watcher abruptly pulled his head down below the land, and he realized that he was looking at the perfect defensive position against men riding uphill. If the badmen had left

160

two or three of their company up there to cover their wake against possible pursuit, Gunn and his ranchmen could easily be ambushed and wiped out if they rode onwards and eventually tried to force the crest.

Having received a hint of what could be, Gunn knew that it was unthinkable to take even the slightest risk of being surprised in this manner and, seeing the line of the town trail down to the east of him and about a mile and a half away, he shouted the change of course to his companions and then yanked his mount's head to the left, dipping now for the lower country and travelling the nearer lip of the hollow beneath the climb that he had just shunned. Inevitably, questions were voiced at his back — and there were one or two yells of protest — but Gunn had no doubt that Forbes had already perceived the point of his action and would know what to say to quiet the foolish or reckless.

In fact no such words were necessary,

and Gunn knew that he had made the right decision when a splutter of firing off the height opposite told of an ambush thwarted and frustrated men left at a loose end. But the shooting was inaccurate and soon stopped, and after that it was once more a matter of riding to the demands of the land. The descent had the odd bad patch — in terms of rock and mire — but once that was over it flattened comfortably enough to its end, and Gunn and his followers had only to swing their horses to the right when they reached the trail and resume heading directly for Blackford.

Again the rumbling of hooves was the only sound that accompanied the party. Gunn maintained the rate of progress by forcing his will through the beast beneath him. But for the second time during this ride the pace was beginning to tell, and the horses throughout the Link B-G band were patched with lather and starting to dip their noses. Yet there could be no let up, for speed was the only weapon that could thwart the evil that might be shaping ahead.

Now the ranch party was within two miles of town, and the rooftops and church spire were visible across the flat before them. Then a popping of shots became audible, the echoes reaching high, and Gunn knew that he had anticipated correctly and felt a definite relief in recognising that he had shown a leader's judgment throughout. Not that he was in any sense pleased by what he could hear, for it probably meant that Blackford's wealth was under threat and more men might have to die in order that that threat be removed. But he could not deny himself the basic satisfaction that, put to it, he had led a body of men who were used to sound captaincy in a manner which they could hardly complain of. It augured well for the future. As the boss of the Link B-G, he would have to prove himself up to his station; and he believed that he had come through the first test.

The horses were scrambling a little now, but the gallop persisted, and a few more minutes did it. Reaching the limits of the town, they entered the top of the main street. Gunn strained his eyes towards the middle of the place, for the bank was situated there — just beyond the Barkworth Hotel and on the right — and, from a hundred and fifty yards out, he had the vision of two men standing outside the grey stone building and holding half a dozen horses between them, while threatening the empty ground about them with six-shooters held in their right hands.

Their attentions fixing on the riders pounding in from the north, this pair instinctively sank at the knees and waited for Gunn and company to get closer. They opened fire at a range of forty yards. Gunn plucked out his Colt and triggered an answer, and the revolvers of the men riding behind him were not slow to add to the response. It became blast and counter-blast, and the racket in the street developed a dinning quality — through which the snorting of frightened horses made crazy music — and the vibrations pulsed between walls, forcing north and south of their origins. The mounts held by the two villains sensed panic elsewhere and began to rear and dance, forcing their minders to cease shooting and fight with both hands to hold them down. Then one of the outlaws received a hit. He fell, limbs threshing, and his companion — appearing to sense his own end in that of the first man — virtually gave up his task and stared wide-eyed at the charging ranch hands, bearing a charmed life as bullets flew about him; but suddenly a black hole manifested above the bridge of his nose, and he toppled to the ground and lay motionless.

At that moment three more of the outlaws appeared on the scene. They came running out of the bank with what looked like empty saddlebags slung over their left shoulders. The man at the centre of the trio held but a single Colt, while those on either side of him grasped a pistol in each hand.

They looked towards Gunn and the cowboys, instantly realizing what had happened, and then their eyes sought their horses and, seeing the minders down and the brutes scattered, they seemed to recognise that only a supreme effort on their part would give them any chance at all; so they gritted their teeth and stood their ground, triggering fast, and chaplets of smoke pulsed away from their sixguns as they set up a deadly fire that instantly emptied a saddle or two at Gunn's back.

Gunn reined in only yards short of the spitting muzzles, and his followers skidded-to all around. Erect in his hull, it seemed to him that flame stabbed directly into his face, and he was conscious of hot lead virtually singeing the stubble on his left cheek. Gazing into the moon-face of the outlaw who had so nearly killed him, Gunn withered the man with his eyes and then sent him reeling backwards with a slug through the body. Then the tallest of the trio before the bank turned on

166

Gunn. He swept his revolvers into line, thumbs squeezing back the hammers, but Gunn got in just ahead of him, and his bullet struck the top of the tall man's right shoulder and sent him staggering, his pistols ribboning at the sky. He made a valiant effort to recover himself, but lead from weapons other than Gunn's pierced his vitals, and he fell with no more than a despairing gasp. The last man of the three faced up to it gamely, but the odds against him were too great, and the expression of life on his face seemed to become one of death at the snapping of finger and thumb.

Jumping off his horse, Gunn cast rapid glances about him. Five badmen had just fallen, but Alec Striker had not been among them. Where was the man? He had to be somewhere close by, since there could be little doubt that it had been his mind which had planned the reversal of the outlaws' flight and the swoop on Blackford's bank. If he wasn't out here, he was most probably still inside, and Gunn saw no choice but to go into the building and look for the man.

Springing onto the sidewalk, Gunn moved to the three low steps that gave access to the bank's front door. Ascending the brick risers, he shouldered through the twin leaves of woodwork above them and dodged swiftly to his right, Colt at the ready and shoulder-blades rubbing the wall behind him as he peered into the sepia light of the big room before him, both seeking Alec Striker's shape and expecting a revolver to flash at him from the shadows in the direction of the grilles at any instant now.

But there was no shot, and no Alec Striker either. The man clearly wasn't in the bank's public space. Now Gunn ran towards the counters. Reaching the long divide, he lifted on tiptoe and peered through the grilles at the floor behind the desks on the other side. He saw three tellers lying there, and judged that they had been knocked on the head and were presently unconscious. Then, at the extreme right end of the divide, he saw a wicket, and this had undoubtedly been unlocked at the beginning of the raid to assist the thieves in their task of emptying the money boxes under the counters.

Gunn ran to the wicket. He passed through it at top speed. After satisfying himself that the tellers on the floor were indeed still alive, he made for the door that stood open in the wall at the back of the bank's main room and stepped into the passage behind it which penetrated towards the building's rear. Here he saw two open doors — one in the wall to his left, and the other in that to his right. The one to his left carried a brass plate and the legend that it was the manager's office, while that on the right was obviously a staff room of lesser importance. The manager's office was empty, but the staff room was occupied by a pair of stenographers. The ladies were ashen-cheeked and shaking with fear, and it was obvious that they had recently been advised of what their fates would be if they opened their mouths or stirred a muscle. "Where's he gone, ladies?" Gunn snapped; but realized at once that he could hardly have addressed them in tones less likely to produce a reply; and, smiling, he softened his voice and said: "I'm with the good guys. It's all over. You're safe. All I want to know is where Alec Striker has gone. I'm after him, d'you see?"

The younger of the two women, a fat, pink-cheeked blonde, with pale blue eyes and the suspicion of a goitre, shrugged square in her new gingham dress and let out a shuddering sigh. Then she gulped and said: "He used the back door, and took Mr Edison along to unlock it for him."

"Thanks," Gunn said. "Take it easy now."

"Don't leave — " the blonde began.

But Gunn had already left the doorway of the staff room. He moved on down the passage. Now he came to

170

another door. This he unlatched, then thrust wide open with the sole of his left boot, peering beyond it to left and right before entering a room which appeared to contain the staff facilities — a table, chairs, washbasins, cupboards, shelves, and a stove — while in the wall at its back and directly before him, was a door that stood half-open into a rear yard.

Crossing the room, Gunn paused at the back door and peeped round the jamb. He saw a man of large head and ample proportions lying inert to the right of the threshold. A nasty contusion on the bald whiteness of the other's crown betrayed that he had shared the fate of the tellers and been struck unconscious by a blow from a gun barrel. Gunn knew the motionless figure for George Edison, the manager of the bank and, realizing that he could do little or nothing to help the man, simply stepped outside and walked round him, then headed for the open gate that he could see ahead of him in the wall that bordered the northern side of the bank's back yard.

Passing through the gateway, Gunn made an instinctive left turn and sprinted, heading out onto the path that ran along the foot of the lots on this side of town. Here he checked and, gazing to his right, spotted, about a hundred and fifty yards beyond him, the figures of Alec Striker and Marissa Coates. Both were running flat out, the man in front and the girl pursuing. Marissa had gathered her hems high about her thighs and was revealing a fine pair of legs as she dashed up the narrow way. The couple were in view for about a second only, then made the sharpest of right turns and disappeared into what the watcher judged to be the back yard of the girl's home.

Gunn smiled grimly to himself. The pair had been in too much of a hurry; they ought to have looked back. Well, he figured he had them, for it looked as if Marissa meant to hide Striker in her mother's house for the time being. Doubtless she intended to put him on a horse later on — perhaps after night had fallen — and send him off to whatever place of safety he had decided upon. Whatever the fact of that — and how she had come to be so propitiously placed to help him just now — they were unlikely to be leaving home again in the next few minutes, and that would be long enough to meet his, Gunn's, needs.

Facing right, he followed the path up the foot of the lots at an easy walk, breathing deeply to recover his breath, for he wished to be absolutely steady when he sprang his surprise on Alec and Marissa. He also took the opportunity of reloading his Colt as he moved along, and by the time he reached the spot where the couple had recently made their turn, his lungs were behaving normally and his pistol was charged in all six chambers.

The back yard of the Coates's home was enclosed by a fence of wooden boards that was about five feet high. Gunn looked over the western section of this fencing and passed an eye along the rear of the house. He saw that the drapes had been drawn at the downstair windows. While the reason for this was obvious enough, he saw it as far more to his advantage than that of the pair indoors — since they had plainly left themselves no holes to peep through — and he quietly opened the gate and openly approached the back of the dwelling, coming to a halt outside the kitchen door.

He considered the latch a moment, then lifted it with a steady hand and gave the woodwork a tiny push inwards — to break any adhesions between door and frame — and the way inside opened silently to him. Moving into the entrance, he stood and listened, but all was still, though he could hear the voices of Alec and Marissa, kept low, drawing to him from the parlour behind the rear wall of the kitchen into which he now stepped fully, catfooting then to the partially open door more or less opposite that served the living-room from the back of the house.

Halting again, he stood behind the opening, body rigid and ears once more straining, and now he could just make out what was being said. He instantly detected a note of argument present, for it seemed that Striker was reminding the girl that he and his brothers were less than welcome in Montana while she was insisting that their transgressions had belonged to a past decade, and that age, coupled to small artificial or natural changes in their appearances, would make life up there safe enough provided they kept out of the larger town in the less wild and woolly southern third of the territory. "I think you may be right about that, girl," Gunn heard Alec Striker admit somewhat reluctantly. "A mite of facial hair and a change in the side a man wears his parting can alter his physiog no end and it is nigh ten years since me and my brothers pulled that bank job up in Bozeman. But there's a heap more doing in Colorado and New Mexico, and I've always had a yen to travel down the Rio Grande into Texas. South's best, I reckon."

"You only see what you want to see," came Marissa's now openly impatient rejoinder. "It's a matter of the distances involved, Alec. After what you've done here today gets fully understood, you're going to become all kinds of a wanted man in Wyoming. It was the maddest thing to ride back to Blackford and try to rob the bank! Where would you have been now if I hadn't been lucky enough to correctly anticipate what might go wrong and where you might flee the building?"

"Okay, you're a wonder, honey," Striker agreed, half sincere but also half mocking.

"You are an ingrate, Alec!" Marissa protested bitterly. "But we must not quarrel about that. It's vital we keep to the point. There are just a few miles between us and the Montana line, whereas we have three hundred miles of Wyoming to the south of us. Pretty soon the telegraph key will be clicking away, and the sheriffs in places like Casper and Rawlins and Laramie will be hearing that you are to be arrested on sight. It would be madness to go south and risk all that when there's little danger to travelling north."

"You make a good argument, Marissa," Striker growled, "but it isn't what I want."

"If you won't think about yourself, think about me!"

"You don't have to come with me. It's your idea."

"I'm coming!"

"Then you do it my way," Striker retorted flatly. "I have bank money in those saddlebags down beside the couch. I picked up all that was going when we cleaned up in Edison's place. I figure I might make something of that cash south of here."

"Get wise to yourself, Alec!" Marissa advised. "You're never going to make anything out of any sum of money. You're a spoiler, my love, and will be to the end. The law's organised where you want to go, but it's still scrappy in most of Montana. Mining, and such offer all kinds of easy pickings up north."

"That ain't the fact, honey — "

But Gunn had heard enough. He opened wide the door before him and stepped through into the parlour, where he saw Alec Striker and Marissa Coates sitting together on the couch before an empty fireplace. As they heard his movement, the faces of the pair screwed towards him, their features revealing expressions that were at once startled, baffled and fearful. "Both of you, get your hands up!" Gunn ordered. "You seem to be making a problem of where to go next, Alec. Well, I'm going to solve it for you. You're going to jail!"

"Damn your soul, Gunn!" Striker yelled, leaping to his feet and spinning to face his captor, right hand starting for his revolver.

"No!" Gunn cautioned. "You're dead if you try it, man! It was only out of respect for a friend's living-room that I spared you then!"

Marissa appeared to realize just how far in earnest Gunn was, and she wrapped both her arms around Striker's right arm and hung on with all her strength and weight, making it impossible for the man to even think of reaching for his pistol again. "He will kill you, Alec," she whispered. "I know Jed Gunn. There's not a better man — or a worse one!"

"I'm not going to jail, Gunn," Striker said. "I'm not dragging out my days in a stinking cell."

"Man, you'll be lucky if you don't hang!" Gunn pointed out. "Talk about jail! After those murders at the Barkworth Hotel — because that's what they were — I don't reckon you've got a hope. Hell if I can imagine what kind of hold you may have on Sheriff Lammas, but he won't try to help you after what you've done today. He won't dare! For now, I'm going to lock you in the town jailhouse myself. So make up your mind to it."

Striker's eyes narrowed and grew

calculating; and then his demeanour altered to what seemed a wholly reasonable one. "Can't we do a deal, Gunn?" he asked. "Beside this couch a pair of saddlebags lie. I reckon they contain several thousand dollars. All you have to do is turn your head while we slip away, and the money will be yours. Nor will you ever see Marissa and me again."

"You're even crazier than I thought," Gunn said contemptuously. "Last night you and your brothers tried to lynch me. Today you've murdered a number of ranch hands, and robbed the town bank. That's without all your other crimes, known and unknown. Men like you scare the hell out of me, Striker. I want you out of the society I live in. As for the money, it's going back to where it belongs — the bank." He gestured peremptorily with the muzzle of his Colt. "Unlatch, Alec, and toss your hogleg into the corner of the room behind you and on your left."

Shaking off Marissa's still encumbering

weight, Striker did as he had been told, scowling to himself as his gunbelt thudded down on the boards in the angle of the room to his rear and on the side mentioned.

"Right," Gunn said. "We're going onto the street, and we're going out through the front door." And, moving to his right — one eye on his captives all the time and revolver pointing steadily — he opened the door at the further end of the wall on that hand, which he knew, from his visits in the old days, gave access to the hall. "Get going. You first, Marissa. Nicely. I'm going to let you open the front door. Be careful about it!"

The girl stepped out into the hall. Alec Striker walked after her, and Gunn brought up the rear. His eyes were fixed on his male prisoner's back, as they came to a halt in the hall and stood waiting for Marissa to open the front door, and Gunn was about to speak a hurrying word, when he sensed a movement behind him and instinctively bowed his head to the front. By doing this he unquestionably robbed the gun barrel which scythed across the back of his skull an instant later of much of its force, but he still stopped enough of the blow to fell him, and his consciousness flickered out as his face met the floor and Marissa's laughter pealed a witchlike mockery in his ears.

8

GUNN did not feel that he had been unconscious long as he struggled back to his senses. Nor, though his head ached, was he in any great pain. But he did have awful feelings of defeat and effort wasted. He had had it done, but now he had lost it all again. How had it happened? He hadn't been careless — quite the reverse — and had been sure that he had covered every eventuality. Yet his imagination had stopped just short of the real danger. For it had never occurred to him that there might be somebody else in the house. Somebody upstairs, who must have heard him make his capture and then crept noiselessly down to the hall and stood ready to strike him from behind when he had emerged from the parlour with his prisoners.

He smelled rug dust, and tasted the same, spitting at the vileness of it as he lifted his mouth from the floor and discovered that he had been dragged back into the parlour and dumped in front of the fireplace. Now powerful hands gripped him at the back of his collar and raised upwards and to the rear, dropping him into the armchair on the right of the hearth and so placing him that he sat exactly opposite the fat shape of Zeb Striker, who occupied the second armchair on the left of the grate. Then Alec Striker, who had obviously done the lifting, moved to the rear of the couch and stopped beside Marissa, who was already standing there, her knuckles showing white as she gripped the polished wood along the top of the piece of furniture's high back.

"I figured it must have been you, Zeb," Gunn muttered thickly.

"Made a mistake, did you?" the fat man sneered, crouching towards his left thigh, which held a bloody bandage that was wrapped over his filthy moleskin trousers, and then toying with the gun which rested in his lap. "You bet you made a mistake, mister!"

Seeing everything through a haze, Gunn screwed up his face and massaged his brow.

"He intended to brain you, Gunn," Alec Striker snarled. "You're a lucky man."

"He's an unlucky one," Zeb slavered. "If he hadn't ducked away, it'd be all over for him now. As it is, he's still got it all to come — and I don't aim to spare him much."

"Okay, brother Zeb," Alec said. "I was never a man to spoil another's enjoyment; you amuse yourself as best you can. You can't ride with me and Marissa, that leg being how it is. But try not to use that gun. Shots get heard no matter how hard you try to muffle them, and the girl and me don't want any suspicion called to this house until we're miles and miles away."

"Do my best," Zeb pouted. "Got a knife on my hip with an edge to shave a billy goat. When I run that round Gunn's throat, there won't be hardly a mark to show, but I'll lift his head off by the cowlick. You see if I don't." He jerked a thumb towards the back door. "The light's wanin', boy. You and Marissa slide off. Get yourself a change of hoss — after you and her have doubled up out to our ranch. Leave this here killin' to me. I'm aching for it. It sure is owing!"

"Quit the moaning," Alec said coldly. "You've been hurt before. Just don't go and foul up now, Zeb. It's important to give Gunn his quietus. With him under the sod, there's no voice about here to greatly fear, and us Strikers may be able to come back to our ranch some day."

"I'm as little likely to foul up here," said fat Zeb arrogantly, jerking his thumb once more — though this time at a higher angle and into the west, "as Dan is likely to over yonder. Knowing him, I bet he'll help himself to a cut or two of what's good before he turns what's left of Grace Tucker over to the buzzards."

"Who cares?" Alec asked indifferently. "Just so long as the blonde bitch is dead and folk know our revenge is to be feared." He grinned ferociously down at Marissa. "Only a girl, ain't she? Pick up that bank money!"

"Just a girl," Marissa agreed, looking uncomfortable and emitting a sigh as she picked up the saddlebags containing the stolen money from beside the couch.

"You get more agreeable, miss!" Alec Striker gritted, seeming suddenly angered by his lady love's attitude. "There's no other way. You're either with us or against us. Folk only respect what they fear. Ain't that the truth, Gunn? You tell her!"

"I'll tell her nothing," Gunn said disdainfully.

"She knows what you are; and you can see that she knows. A man as black-hearted as you've become, Alec, must be nearing the end of his string. I don't know how it will come, and I can't tell what shape it will take, but there's a justice that will overtake you before long."

"You don't say!" Alec Striker jeered.

"I do say," Gunn responded soberly.

Alec Striker opened his mouth to say something more, but Gunn's words — or the manner in which they had been uttered — seemed to have had a more profound effect on him than might have been expected; for he closed his mouth again and looked uneasy; then, seizing Marissa by her right arm, he thrust her in the direction of the kitchen, meeting her protests and awkward footing with a still more determined force, and then he and the girl disappeared into the kitchen and his voice called: "Slay me that croaking raven, Zeb! And goodbye, brother!"

Zeb flinched, toadlike in his chair and the fading light through the closed drapes. "Don't you say 'goodbye'!" he shouted. "Don't use that word! It's so long. Say 'so long', Alec!"

But the only reply Zeb received was

the noise of the back door shutting; then, his yellow teeth bared, the fat man glowered at Gunn. "Why'd you do it?" he demanded.

"Do what?" Gunn countered, sensing now that he had brought some kind of superstitious atmosphere into being.

"What you did."

"I did nothing," Gunn replied. "I spoke some words, that's all. If there was anything else, it was in your minds. Or maybe we're being overlooked. Perhaps Grace Tucker is better protected by the Spirits than you know. Folk who dwell in the woods develop powers. Grace has got a powerful friend among men who are not quite as we are."

"Don't talk such rubbish!" the fat man scoffed. "Do you figure us Strikers haven't kept a casual eye on that yellow-haired girl across the years. You're talking about that old coot, Roarin' Bear, ain't you? We know she's pally with him. He's just a flea-bit old fool of a redskin chief, with an eye to a white girl." The blubber vibrated across Zeb's huge shoulders as he laughed derisively. "We know all about Roarin' Bear!"

"Does he know *all* about you, Zeb?"

"If he did?" Zeb Striker asked. "What'd he do, Gunn? Us whites have them copper-skinned varmints where we want them these days. We string them up by the neck if they try playing Hob, how they once did."

"Sounds like the Strikers," Gunn observed. "The lynch rope is never far from your reckoning."

"We have our little ways, Gunn," Zeb admitted. "You were lucky last night, and you've been lucky most of the day, but now your luck's run out." Pistol cocked and pointing across the hearth, he leaned forward now and drew a big hunting knife from the scabbard on his left hip. "Talk's for the friendly, mister, and we've been talkin' too much. It's time we got your throat cut, and I got back upstairs to rest this leg."

"You won't fire that gun," the captive said with a confidence he didn't feel.

"Yes, I will," the fat man gloated.

"You force me to it, and I'll shoot you straight in the guts. Ain't no shock like a bullet in the guts. You'll lie there all stricken, and I'll step up and draw this edge across your throat. Boy, will the blood fly."

"Butcher!" Gunn mocked. "Pig, too. Have you no manners?"

"Hey?" Zeb demanded, shocked out of his malicious delight. "What are you saying?"

"This is Mrs Coates's home," Gunn answered craftily. "She's going to be a relation of yours, isn't she? Are you the kind of fellow who messes up a lady's parlour so that she can't live in it? How do you think she'd feel about you Strikers if she came home and found me lying on the hearth in a pool of my own blood?"

"There's no chance Gwen Coates is going to light on your body," Zeb retorted. "I aim to hide your remains in the stable out on the lots until such time as I have the chance to dig a hole and bury you."

"So the stable's the place to do the dirty work!" Gunn declared. "You shame your family, Zeb — you really do!"

"Drat it, Gunn!" the fat man howled indignantly. "I ain't some kid in knee-britches!"

"Sorry," Gunn apologised. "My mistake. It was just that you were behaving like one."

Zeb Striker struggled erect, his face contorting with pain. "You get on your feet!" he bellowed. "I've had enough of you, Jed Gunn. There's the kitchen door. Get your ass through it! I know how to conduct myself in somebody else's house — and you'll bleed out just the same, stable or parlour."

Gunn heaved himself to the vertical. The ceiling swooped at him and the room spun, but he managed to keep upright. Then, amazed at how well his simple play on Zeb's pride had worked, he lurched past the other and made for the entrance to the kitchen, aware that, although he was far from entirely fit himself, he must have a considerable advantage over the wounded man, whose stiffened leg and great burden of excess flesh were rendering him far short of fully mobile. Gunn also realized that he must capitalise on his advantage while it was at its maximum, for Zeb's ability to get about would improve quickly once he began forcing his body into action.

The risk had to be taken, and it might as well be taken now. Giving the impression that he was feeling even worse than was the case, Gunn walked slowly and with head bowed. He squared shakily into the kitchen doorway; then, coming abruptly to life, went through the opening like a man on spring-heels. Landing lightly on the other side of the threshold, he spun round and slammed the door shut, throwing his weight against it and holding the latch down.

Ignoring Zeb Striker's sudden shout of wrath, Gunn felt the fat man's enormous weight drive against the woodwork and then the pressure of the other's presence increase as he put out his strength. "Let me through, damn your eyes!" Striker roared. "I'll plug you through the g'damned wood if you don't!"

That was it. Zeb, driven past a certain point, would fire his gun; but, out of fear of his brother Alec's wishes, he would not do it until he was sure he could not regain control of the situation anyhow else. Until that moment, he would huff and puff and keep shoving with all his might and main; but in the process he would almost certainly lose sight of the danger to himself in what he was doing — and that was the instant that Gunn was working for.

"I've got you placed exactly!" the fat man raved. "A slug will easily pierce the door and drop you! Let me through! You hear me, mister?"

Still Gunn kept silent, employing all his breath and muscle to resist the fat man's pressure, and his head was almost bursting with strain as he assessed the exact state of Zeb's mounting rage and frustration. Then, suddenly convinced that the other was about to shoot, Gunn sprang back from the woodwork and let it fly open; and the fat man, taken by surprise, flew into the kitchen with it, crossing the entire width of the floor and ramming his head against the room's rear wall, from whence he rebounded to the floor and lay sprawled upon his back.

Standing on Zeb's left, Gunn was amazed to see that the fat man, through it all, had managed to retain his hold on the knife in his left hand and the revolver in his right. Both were deadly weapons — and both could kill quickly but the pistol was the more to be feared of the two; and, since he could hardly hope to disarm Zeb on both sides with the move that he essayed next, Gunn decided in his split second of preparation that the Colt must be his target.

Into the air he bounded, drop kicking, and the toe of his right boot tore the revolver out of the fat man's grasp and sent it spinning to the further end of the room, where it hit the wall and fell to the floor. Landing beyond Zeb, Gunn let his original impetus carry him into a staggering stride and then a headlong dive towards the weapon. He came to rest on top of the six-shooter and clawed it into his grasp, rolling then to his left, the movement bringing him into a sitting position against the wall which had previously checked the pistol's flight.

Triumphant, Gunn expected to find himself with at least a moment in hand over whatever aggressive action Zeb might next attempt, but he received another shock, for the fat man had somehow managed to sit up and make a turn on his ungainly posterior that had brought him face to face with the man who had become his adversary. And more. He had transferred the knife to his right hand and was now holding it by its tip and ready to throw.

The Colt in Gunn's hand was cocked. He raised the weapon the necessary inch or two and pulled the trigger, and lead left the sixgun's muzzle in an eruption of smoke and flame. Zeb's eyes blinked, and his jaw dropped, but the knife remained poised and his arm retained all the strength that was needed for the cast.

Gunn let fly again. He could see no means of sparing the monster across the room from him and simply fanned off his weapon's three remaining bullets. At such short range, he could hardly miss and knew that each shot had gone home; and for that reason he could hardly credit his eyes when, looking out through the thinning gunsmoke, he saw Zeb still sitting as before, the hunting knife held between finger and thumb and the same murderous intent in his stare. It seemed that the fat man must still make his throw, and Gunn got ready to try to dodge the blade; but all at once Zeb grunted, the knife fell from his grip, and he reeled loosely to the rear and measured his length upon the kitchen floor, belly grotesquely piled and heels gently drumming on the big square of coconut matting that lay between the cook's table and the sink.

Rising, Gunn walked slowly over to Zeb Striker's quivering mass. Halting at Zeb's feet, he gazed down on the man who had planned to kill him, unloading the fired shells from this his second appropriated Colt of the day as he did so; then, the weapon once more being a forty-four calibre, he reloaded it from his gunbelt and thrust it into his holster, giving the now motionless Zeb a kick in the heel with his left toe. The fat man did not stir, but went on grinning sightlessly at the ceiling. He was as dead as he was ever going to be and, again without pity for a Striker deceased, Gunn turned away from the corpse and stepped back into the gloom of the parlour.

Going to the window, he parted the drapes and looked out onto the main street, where the scene was full of shadows and lines were losing their sharpness in the evening light. But out there he did see something that he had rather feared he might see. Folk were assembling on the sidewalk across the way and whispering among themselves as they gazed towards the Coates's house. It meant that the noise of the shots fired indoors had been heard outside. While he did not wish to hide his presence, he also did not want to be forced into making public explanations right now. Thus he went through to the hall and opened the front door. Then he stepped outside onto the street and closed up behind him, turning right and pointedly ignoring the people opposite as he did so.

He walked in the direction of the bank, and had covered about half the distance involved, when he spotted men dressed in range garb legging it towards him and recognised them as Ray Forbes and the surviving cowboys of the Link B-G crew. "Where have you been, boss?" Forbes asked hoarsely from a dozen yards away. "We've been looking for you all over the place!"

"Now you've found me," Gunn advised, a hand signal enjoining calm; and Forbes stopped at the moment that they met and faced round, picking up the step and walking down the street beside him; and the other runners checked appropriately and did the same, falling in behind their boss and the foreman.

"What happened?" Forbes asked.

"I chased Alec Striker," Gunn explained. "He left the bank through the back door. Marissa Coates met him. She took him to her house." He went on to tell the rest in the same terse manner, ending: "It figures Alec Striker and Marissa left the lots doubling on the girl's horse. They've gone to the Striker ranch so that Alec can pick up a mount. I reckon they'll be filling a sack with provisions too. It isn't so long since that pair left town. If we gallop out to the Striker place real fast, there's a chance we may even now catch them before they leave for Montana."

They had by now reached the bank, and were standing between the rails to which all the Link B-G horses — including Gunn's and those belonging to the ranch's dead and wounded — had been tied.

"I caught yours and put him with the rest," Forbes said.

"Obliged," Gunn responded. "Have you had any contact with the law?"

"No," the foreman answered. "I guess the sheriff is still out of town. Wonder what's keeping him?"

"Oh, I'm disposed to be charitable," Gunn said sourly, "and say that Satan looks after his own."

Gunn went to his horse, freed it and stepped up. The ranch hands did likewise. Then Gunn led into the alley that ran down the northern side of the bank, and they rode out to the grass beyond the lots and visions of the now dusky spread of country that rolled out to the site of the Striker buildings and then onwards to join up with the pastures of the Link B-G.

Disregarding the hard use that he had already inflicted on his horse, Gunn kicked for a gallop and kept his heels digging away. Head and shoulders bent over his mount's neck, he travelled between south and west, and it wasn't many minutes later when the Striker property showed up ahead, blacker than the blackness of the range against the single pale bar of the afterglow that lingered in the western sky.

Hoofbeats rumbling and making no attempt to hide their presence, the ranch party crossed the intervening land at the same all-out gallop, and the ranch buildings came on apace; and there in the gloaming, outside the front door of the house, Gunn perceived the figures of Alec Striker and Marissa Coates. The couple had been about to mount the two horses standing at the house hitching rail, but now they craned towards the sound of the oncoming Link B-G riders and, after a moment of high-pitched talk, appeared to accept that they would be almost immediately overtaken if they swung up and attempted to flee. Suddenly they

202

sprang away from their mounts and ran indoors, and Gunn was near enough to hear the front door shutting and the retaining beam falling into place. Now he put pressure on the bit and brought the pace of his horse down to a heavily checked trot. "Surround the place!" he shouted at his followers. "Watch all the windows and doors they might try to escape from!"

A rifle flashed from a window to the right of the front door, and another blazed from a position almost beside it. Gunn felt a small object flick his left sideburn, and the second bullet whipped the top of his pommel and went whirring to the earth, leaving a faint stink of burned leather behind it.

"You keep your distance!" Alec Striker's voice warned from the house. "Is that you, Gunn?"

Jumping to the ground, Gunn prudently put the head and shoulders of his horse between him and the Winchesters in the windowspace. "It's me Alec," he acknowledged.

"That great fat — !"

"He's dead," Gunn interrupted.

"I knew the lummox would foul up!" Striker declared, sounding more than a trifle hysterical. "I knew it, I knew it, I knew it!"

"So you knew it," Gunn said laconically. "How about blaming yourself? There's not much forecast in leaving a wounded man to kill a fit and desperate one, Alec. You Strikers are all a sight too confident." He paused, asking himself how best to get this over quickly — yet doubting that it could be. "Look, boy! I'm appealing to your good sense. We've got you dead to rights. Are you coming out?"

"I'll see you in hell first!" Striker scorned.

"You're going to get killed."

"I'll take a few of you with me."

"In this light?"

"Whatever light."

"Okay," Gunn said judiciously. "That's your choice. Send Marissa out. You don't want her to end up dead as well, do you?"

"I'm staying with him!" the girl's voice declared. "If he dies, I die!"

"Are you playing it crafty, Marissa?" Gunn inquired. "Don't think we won't open fire if you elect to stay in there."

"Fire away!" the girl said defiantly.

"He isn't worth it," Gunn advised.

"That's for me to decide, Jed," Marissa said in quieter tones, "and I think he is."

"Romantic poppycock, you silly girl!" Gunn shouted in exasperation. "You heard what he really is while we were in your parlour. What he said of Grace Tucker goes for you too. You're just a girl."

"Is it that you talk a good fight, Gunn?" Alec Striker demanded in a bored voice. "Or are you bent on talking us to death?"

"Last chance," Gunn bit in reply. "Are you coming out of there, Marissa?"

"No!" the girl flung back, sending a bullet after the word, and Gunn's horse emitted a frightened snort and went skittering to the rear as the tiny missile flew past its nose.

"Very well!" Gunn shouted, moving after his horse and seizing its trailing reins. "On your own head be it!"

9

DIGGING in his heels, Gunn regained control of his horse, then called on Forbes to give the order to open fire.

"Pour it in, boys!" the foreman shouted. "Pass the word round back! Shoot as you see your chances!"

Four or five cowboys had formed a loose half-circle about the front of the house while Gunn had been talking to its occupants. Now these men, still sitting their mounts, began to shoot. Muzzles blazed in the twilight, and bullets sped towards the window which Alec Striker and the girl were defending. Holding his horse at the bit, Gunn heard glass raining down and wood splintering. The fire was fierce and obviously accurate and, while he had formed the impression that the Striker ranch house — ignoring its present state of neglect — had been strongly built and could absorb a lot of punishment, he nevertheless felt that the kind of penetrating fire to which the defenders were being subjected must soon produce a casualty — if only by ricochet — and, knowing how these things had the grim habit of turning out, he feared that it would be the inexperienced and somewhat reckless girl who stopped lead.

He had believed earlier that the prospect would leave him cold; but now that it was here, he found that there was something in him that could not let it happen. It seemed to him that suddenly Marissa was doing the right thing for the wrong reasons. In the name of love she was prepared to sacrifice her life for a man who was quite worthless. Today she had transgressed against him and others, but this devotion was proof enough that the devil had not yet claimed her soul entirely. For the sake of Gwen Coates, the girl's mother, his own remembered fondness of yesteryear, and the bit of good that remained in her, he could not let Marissa die like some harridan of the Owlhoot. If she would not come out, he must go indoors. Perhaps he could find a satisfactory solution in there. It would mean placing himself in extreme danger, but he felt that it must be done.

Letting go of his horse, Gunn peered about him in the twilight. He wanted to tell Ray Forbes what he had in view, but found it impossible to pick the man out from the several horsemen jockeying in the vicinity. He opened his mouth to call the foreman's name, but shut it again, fearing that he might alert the couple in the house to the possibility that he was on the scheme. Thus he decided to keep quiet and attempt what he had in mind regardless of what friend and foe alike were doing. While so engaged, there would be the chance of getting shot at by his own people; but he felt the risk justifiable in the circumstances; and, bending low, he flitted towards the house, merging with the deep shadows along its northern end and then creeping to a point in the wall beyond where he could just make out glass dully shining.

He was looking for a window, and this was one sure enough. A quick examination, mainly tactile, revealed that the glass had been firmly shut, though whether or not it had been locked on the inside he could not as yet tell. Clearly this was what he must find out next and, placing his hands on either side of the frame — since he was fairly sure that he was dealing with a sash — he bunched his arms and shoulders and forced upwards. Perhaps a trifle to his surprise, the frame slid some way up the sash with reasonable freedom, though it did emit a shrill squeak or two at the start and, fearing that his effort to force an entry might have been overheard, he crouched low and pressed his forehead against the windowsill, listening hard, but there was no movement inside the building and he soon decided that it was safe to continue with his break-in.

Rising to his full height, hands in position again, he forced the window as far upwards as it would go; then, raising his left leg, he thrust it across the sill and brought down his hands to rest upon this piece of woodwork. After that he ducked his head and rolled to his left and into the room beyond, drawing his right foot to join the other on bare floorboards and then straightening up to breathe the heavy atmosphere of what was probably a bedroom.

He stood rigidly, an ear cocked down the length of the house. The two rifles in use within the building were still exploding regularly, and he formed the impression — from the absorption of sound — that there was a hall between the room in which he stood and the one in which Alec Striker and the girl were firing their Winchesters. Assuming the presence of the space, he was delighted that it was there, for he was going to have to strike a match and crawl around a little to find out what was available to him in here, and the presence of the gap and the walls that contained it would cut off the two defenders from all traces of the light and any sounds that he might make.

Gunn dropped to his knees. Then he fished out a match and set its sulphur tip flaring with a flick of his thumbnail. Holding the small light as high as he dared, he gazed slowly around him, taking in the huge and dirty-looking bed which dominated most of the room and giving a grunt of satisfaction as his eyes came to rest on the top of a chest-of-drawers and the object that he had been seeking most: an oil lamp. Even from his present position he could see that the lamp had a glass reservoir that was almost full of what looked like paraffin, and he was pretty certain that he could make good use of some of that oil.

Creeping across the room, his match still flickering, Gunn came to the chest-of-drawers and halted at its foot. Then he reached down the oil lamp which he had previously seen, shaking out what was left of his match at the same time and, working in the dark now, unscrewed the lamp's top, lifting away the glass chimney and the brass base to which it was fitted. The sodden wick left the reservoir in the same process and dribbled its stinking contents onto Gunn's thighs, but he ignored the reeking wetness and carefully placed the bits and pieces on the floor to his left. After that he untied his neckerchief and rolled it into the shape of candle, carefully feeling for the lamp's reservoir again and then feeding the shaped material into its top, pressing down further and further until he was sure that the entire neckerchief was drenched with oil. Then, laying the bandanna aside, he groped around in the blackness again, putting the lamp back together, and that done, he rummaged out a second match and lighted the wick, quickly trimming it to provide himself with a permanent means of seeing about.

There was a door in the wall against which the chest-of-drawers stood. This exit was situated to the left of the piece of furniture, and Gunn opened it now without rising. Then, picking up the lamp in his left hand and the saturated bandanna in his right, he crawled silently out of the doorway and found himself in the hall whose presence he had mooted, noting almost at once in the lamplight to his right and in the wall on the opposite side of the space — a door that undoubtedly served the room which Alec Striker and Marissa Coates were at present defending.

Creeping obliquely across the hall, Gunn stopped a little to the left of the door on which his gaze had lately settled and placed his lamp well clear of the entrance on the same hand, turning aside now and striking a third match, the flame of which he held to the more tightly rolled end of the candle-shaped neckerchief which he had soaked in lamp oil. Within moments the paraffin drenched material caught fire, and Gunn jacked himself upright and moved square with the door behind which Striker and the girl were sheltering. Then he lifted the latch and flung the woodwork open, casting the now brightly flaring neckerchief towards the front of the room beyond — where he knew the pair were at bay before the window — and, fanned by its rapid passage through the air, the oil-soaked bandanna softly exploded into a fireball and landed just short of the kneeling pair, unquestionably blinding them with the brightness of its presence and leaving Gunn in what to their eyes could only be the darkness behind the blaze.

Gunn drew his revolver and thumbed back its hammer. "Drop the rifles!" he ordered.

Marissa obeyed instantly, scared orbs staring out of a face that seemed to have aged abruptly by twenty years, but Alec Striker bounded to his feet and, though clearly unable to mark his target, let fly in the direction of the doorway. The bullet passed over Gunn's right shoulder, missing him by perhaps an inch, and he triggered an instant response, intending to kill, but his slug made contact with some portion of Striker's Winchester and tore the weapon out of the other's hands screeching thereafter into audible contact with the ceiling.

Striker swore, but did not lose his presence of mind, and he dropped to the floor again and caught Marissa Coates to him with his left arm, rising once more with her in the position of a shield. Then, whipping out his revolver with his right hand, he fired twice towards the doorway, one of the bullets burying itself in the wall on Gunn's left, the other splitting the door jamb and casting splinters everywhere; but Gunn had already stepped to his right and into the cover of the wall on that side, while remaining so placed that he could still see Striker and the girl down a very acute angle. "You're still caught, you damned coward!" he advised.

"We'll see!" Striker rapped in reply. "Tell those half-wits outside to stop shooting!"

"Or else — what?"

"I'll shoot Marissa!"

"Your sweetheart!" Gunn returned in utter contempt. "I thought that would be it!"

"I mean to live seventy years, Gunn," Striker sneered. "Shout — or Marissa won't live another second!"

Cupping his left hand to his mouth, Gunn bawled at the top of his voice: "Hold your fire, men!"

The shooting from the night spluttered out, and it was followed by a tense silence.

"You've got the idea, Gunn," Striker said. "Get out there and join those a dollar-a-day loons. Place a horse close to the door and ready for me. And remember — just a hint of treachery and the girl gets a hole blown in her!"

"Alec!" Marissa protested, her voice hollow and disbelieving. "Oh, Alec!"

"Shut up!" Striker ordered. "Do I get what I want, Gunn? Or does Marissa get a bullet?"

Though infuriated by how things had turned out, the decent man in Gunn remained uppermost. Striker was calling the tune, and he had no choice but to play it; so, crossing the doorway — and perceiving as he did so that the oil-soaked neckerchief which he had thrown towards the couple was on the verge of setting the floorboards alight and starting a serious fire — he made for the front door and, pausing there, removed the retaining bar from its iron slots and stood it aside. Then he opened the door and stepped through it, conscious of men and horses before him moving into the reddening fireglow which the room that still held Striker and the girl was now giving out through its ruined window. "Hold it, men!" he ordered. "I'm afraid we've got us a consequence."

"What's on, boss?" Forbes's voice inquired from the gloom on the left.

"Striker's using the girl as a hostage," Gunn called by way of a general explanation. "If she'd got hurt fighting with us, that would have been one thing, but what's happening now is another. We don't want her murder on our hands. Leastways, I don't."

"Son-of-a-bitch!" Forbes growled, advancing into silhouette and sitting tall in the saddle. "You'd have done best to stay out of there."

"Maybe," Gunn said heavily, for he simply could not find it in himself to summon up the heat or indignation that would be needed to tell the foreman he was wrong.

"What's the hold up, Gunn?" came Alec Striker's thunderous inquiry from the back of the hall; and then he triggered a shot that stirred Gunn's hair. "I want that horse!"

"You kill me," Gunn tossed over his

shoulder, "and these guys out here will put paid to you!"

"That won't help the girl," Striker reminded.

Gunn glanced beyond Forbes. He saw his own horse standing much where he had left it. The critter had had a basinful and was tired to the marrow of its bones. Striker had asked for a horse. Why not that one? If he left here on that brute, he wasn't going to travel many miles before it staggered to a halt, and that ought to ensure that he was not too difficult to overtake. Gunn thought the matter over for a single instant more, since it was the only piece of trickery that he could employ in the situation, then made up his mind to employ it.

Without speaking another word to anybody, he strode over to where his horse was drooping and put a hand to its mouth. Then he led the mount across the grass and stood it before the front door of the ranch house. "There's your horse, Striker!" he shouted into the hall. "Come and take it!"

"Stand off!" Alec Striker warned. "All of you!"

"Back away, men," Gunn urged, retreating from the house — where the fire in what he now supposed to be the living-room was a thorough going concern and casting its light several yards in front of the building — and halting beside the brickwork of a shape that he discovered to be a well. Watching the front door of the dwelling, he folded his arms, pistol still in his grasp but the muzzle pointing at the ground. Then, glancing to left and right, he saw that he had been obeyed, and that the Link B-G cowboys, mounted or afoot, had withdrawn to a man and were waiting in much the same semi-relaxed and expectant state as himself.

Still using Marissa as a shield, Alec Striker emerged from the front door of the house a few seconds later and stopped beside the horse. He ordered the girl into the saddle; then, as she climbed astride the mount, swung up behind her, his revolver pressed into her right side all the time. As the pair sat limned against the glow of the fire, Gunn studied them and felt his apprehensions rising, for he could not believe that Striker — who had the saddlebags containing the bank money slung across his right shoulder — had any intention of trying to escape double-mounted, which meant that he was going to dump the girl before they had gone very far. "Striker!" he called.

"What?"

"Set Marissa down."

"And leave myself exposed to your guns?" Striker queried, his features a pale blur as they sought the other speaker in the darkness. "Not blamed likely!"

"I give you my solemn word no shot will be fired at you," Gunn assured him.

"Your solemn word, eh? I'd rather trust what I've got!"

"You harm her, Alec, and I'll chase you past hell-and-gone!"

"Son, you'll chase me anyway!" Striker retorted, then put spurs to hide and set the double burdened horse galloping somewhat ponderously southwards.

"Want for us to give chase, boss?" Forbes called.

"Stay a moment," Gunn answered uncertainly, his eyes fixed upon the receding mount and the figures that weighed it down. Then, as the animal and its riders were about to disappear into the night, a muffled explosion was heard, and the watcher received the impression of a human shape being tipped away from Striker's saddle and bouncing on the ground a couple of times before coming to rest.

"He's shot her!" Forbes announced in tones of disbelief. "The bastard's shot her!"

But Gunn was already in action. Head thrown back, arms tucked in, and legs scissoring, he went for the spot where the body lay at a dead run. The distance might have been a hundred yards, and he covered it in little more than ten seconds. He was aware now of the still young moon swinging up from the east and bringing more light to the countryside than he had realized. Halted beside the figure on the ground, he sank to his knees and heard a faint groan which told him that Marissa was still alive. The girl was lying on her face and cried out in agony when he placed his hands on her shoulders and gently turned her over. He gazed down into her features, but couldn't see much, and fished out another of his matches and scratched fire, holding the small flame towards her and seeing a pair of eyes that were already fading towards the blankness of death. "Who is — ?" she asked dully.

"It's Jed Gunn, Marissa."

"Jed." Her face puckered. "How — how could he?"

"Hold on, girl!" he urged, willing her life to remain within her body. "We'll get you to the doctor just as fast — " But he broke off as he realized that he was talking to eternity; for the girl had already slipped away. Standing up again, he shook out his match and faced round, aware now that panting men already stood about him and that others were hurrying over from the direction of the house.

"Is she dead, boss?"

For a moment Gunn barely grasped that Ray Forbes had spoken to him; and then it came to him that the foreman and others must have dismounted before running here, since no horses were present. "Yes, she's dead, Ray. She spoke a few words to me, then died."

"How can a man do such a thing?" Forbes asked in what had become horrified amazement.

"She couldn't explain it either," Gunn said. "I guess Alec Striker no longer had a use for her."

"Makes you despair of Mankind," the foreman said with a finality that hit bottom but inevitably bounced back. "I know she was a bad girl but — "

"Maybe that's the lesson of it," Gunn

interrupted. "We can't escape what we are because what we are determines what we do."

"Too deep for me, Jed."

"I doubt it, Ray," Gunn said, lifting his eyes and seeing that flames were now licking out of the living-room window of the house and threatening to engulf the dwelling's front wall. "The house is past saving. Talk about a cleansing by fire. Nobody of the Striker name will ever come back to that."

"Guess not."

"I want you to take Marissa Coates's body into town," Gunn said, feeling that he had already lost time enough and must get things moving again. "Hand it to the undertaker. Tell Wally Allen to do the very best he can with the girl — for her mama's sake. The bill is to be sent to the Link B-G."

"We'll see to it," Forbes assured him. "What are you going to do?"

"What you know I'm going to do," Gunn responded. "I've got business to finish with Alec Striker. It shouldn't

226

take me all that long. I put him on a horse that was deadbeat. But expect me back at the ranch when you see me."

"What are you going to do for a horse?"

Gunn didn't bother to answer. He dived through the figures before him and broke into a run again, heading back towards the front of the burning ranch house, where he could see the two horses that Alec Striker and the late Marissa Coates had left tied at the hitching rail. The mounts were now neighing with fear and rearing away from the heat and sparks that the fire adjacent had begun spitting out. Reaching the animals, he freed the brown mare that he knew had belonged to Marissa and then did the same for the big gelding next to it. The male horse was undoubtedly Alec Striker's mount and looked a very good one. Its hide was still patched with dried sweat, and its raked flanks also indicated that it had been hard used during the day, but the brute's head was up and its eye true, and there could be no question that there was still plenty of running left in it. Given the right kind of treatment, it should prove horse enough to bring about its fugitive master's downfall before the night was over, and that ought to be ironical enough for any man.

Mounting up, Gunn yanked the creature's head to the left and pricked the horse into action. He angled across the southern end of the ranch house and, chased briefly by the lancing glow of the flames, galloped out into the dark of the country, the great hush of the miles gathering him and the shimmer of the sickle moon adding its mystery to the softness of the atmosphere.

Presently Gunn came to the trail that edged the northern pastures of the Link B-G. Here he turned right, heading for the not far distant Yellowstone Trail. Then, quite abruptly, he came out of the almost trancelike state that had governed him for a good many minutes past. He realized then that he had been obeying instinct rather than reason, and that — on the memory of what he had overheard Alec Striker saying in Marissa Coates's home an hour or so ago — he could have been acting in error. Striker need not be travelling northwards to the Montana line, but could just as easily be riding south and gratifying his expressed preference for escaping into Colorado, the land of greater opportunities.

This being so, Gunn found himself with the need to ask why he was doing what he was doing, and that meant digging into his subconscious for a minute or so. The result of this self-examination was that he perceived he would soon be turning north himself in recognition that Alec Striker — whatever his evil talents and undoubted strength of character — was a man who had been used to having his brothers around him and had drawn power from the collective wickedness of his family. In the violence of the day, he had lost two brothers and even he could not be so callous as not to have felt something of that loss. Thus, the surviving brother, Dan — who had been sent afield to murder Grace Tucker — would be all the more important to him now, and it was probable that he would head for the woods in the hope of meeting Dan in transit rather than ride south into places where he quite obviously could not hope to meet the man. Which meant that, while the subconscious promptings could not be regarded as a sure guide, they did follow a recognisable logic, and Gunn felt them about as trustworthy as anything that he could pursue.

The land loomed on his right, dim but familiar, and he made out the spot where the Yellowstone Trail left open ground and thrust northwards. He fetched his mount onto the new heading, then cantered steadily between banks which sloped back far and gently on the left but slanted quite abruptly upwards to the outcropping stone of the ridge on his other hand. His progress remained free of hindrance, and the distance between him and the Link B-G pastures began to lengthen, but the very fact of this put another tuck in his confidence; for he was nearing the area in which Grace Tucker lived and had hoped to see or hear something of Alec Striker before now. But he supposed that he must allow for the man's cruelty. Striker was the kind of fiend who would kick the last gasp out of the horse that he was forking; which meant that Gunn would have to travel more miles before he could say with certainty that he had been mistaken in his quarry's intentions after all and that the reasoning processes of his subconscious had played him false.

Gunn increased his concentration. He peered ahead of him with a fixity that made his eyes ache. His horse let out a small grunt at every stride, and beneath him its shoes rang and clattered. The moon glimmered as before, sailing slowly across the heavens at his back, and the high lonesomes bruised the night sky with the blackness of their contours, while the spaces at the earth's edge rose clean and endlessly towards the lowest stars of the ringing firmament. Out of the silence seemed to rock a music that was still more silent, and the spirit of the Ages and things gone hovered in tenuous solution above the stirless treetops, a kind of blanketing awareness that could only brood. Gunn felt utterly alone — lost — thwarted; at his lowest ebb. A man mocked by faith and cheated of purpose. It was all gone. There was just the emptiness of the trail. He might as well turn back, and start again in the morning — or not.

Then, over to his left and not too far away, he heard a rifle bang and another answer it.

10

REINING in, Gunn sat with back straight and head erect, listening. The guns repeated their explosions and the echoes went rolling dully through the peaks of the northwest, a wolfs howl adding a weird endpiece to the racket.

The shooting had to be part of a fight. Dan Striker versus Grace Tucker? Who else could it be? Oh, yes — all things were possible; take nothing for granted. Coincidence was far less coincidental than folk believed, and it was credible — with similar minds having similar thoughts — that there were two more enemies out there bent on seeing each other off. But was it thus? He could not believe it so. His own common sense had to be the ultimate measure. Grace had said that she might go into hiding over Clark's Fork way — in some caves behind an Indian burial ground — and it was highly probable that she had done just that, and that Dan Striker had ultimately found her in this refuge and was now trying to complete the bloody task which had been allotted him. Anyway, Gunn decided that he could not treat this shooting as other than he imagined it to be and that his uncertain pursuit of Alec Striker must end here in favour of doing what he could to help Grace Tucker in her probable difficulties.

The detonations sounded again, one against the other. Then the firing spluttered savagely and became more persistent. Each rifle let go four shots in rapid succession. The echoes set birds stirring in the nearby branches, and one fluttered loudly and squawked a complaint. Gunn frowned at the noise, for he sensed anxiously probing minds yonder and felt the tension that they were feeling as they lived in the knowledge that one mistake could prove their last.

Gunn turned his horse to the left and moved off the trail. He listened in the expectation of hearing further explosions from the gunbattle, but the night was silent again and he was forced to judge his line of travel from his memory of the position of the most recent gunshots which he had heard. Thus, assessing due north on the lie of the Yellowstone Trail, he estimated the direction of his latest movements as approximately north westwards.

He was only a short distance off the beaten way, when he found himself among trees and contact with a low branch warned him that he would be safer on the ground and walking the arboreal darkness. So he swung out of his saddle and, with his horse on lead, began making his way slowly towards the ground from which the detonations had issued.

The start was not good; but, as he penetrated deeper into woods, so greater and greater care was forced on him, for it seemed that a roof had come into being overhead and that black walls now enclosed him on every side. He felt his feet embedding in carpets of moss and pine needles, and there was undergrowth too — some of it thorny and impassable — and he was forced to pass round these obstacles when he encountered them and hope afterwards that he was still moving on course, for he had the underlying fear that he had already lost his sense of direction and had begun wandering aimlessly about the forest; but this uneasiness was largely allayed when another shot split the night, its crisp bark affirming that it had reached him from a point that was now much closer to him than it had been at the time of the earlier firing. Thus he felt reasonably satisfied in his own mind that he was indeed still heading more-or-less straight towards the ground on which the gunbattle was being fought.

Another shot rang in the darkness.

Once more the bangs came nip and tuck. Gunn cursed the night, but imagined that the adversaries were cursing it also. The echoes hammered and vaulted, ringing between distant peaks and rockfaces. Then there was silence again. Gunn pictured furtive shapes skirting back and forth, each seeking the vital moment of advantage, when that single clean shot would bring death to the one and victory to the other. He shuddered as he imagined Grace Tucker throwing up her arms and sinking down in a bloody heap matted with blonde hair. The beauty of her face held the centre of his imagination. His thoughts had hovered about her often during the day, but there had been so much happening that he had not been able to concentrate on her in any meaningful sense.

They had declared themselves partners in revenge, yet their cause — still less than twenty-four hours old — seemed to have become remote and strangely pointless. Everything had developed and changed form, and the simple facts of retribution seemed to have become merged in larger issues and more complex doings. He was about as worried for the woman now as it was in him to be, and the pangs made him wonder at himself. Could there be any real degree of emotional involvement on such short acquaintance? The woman had saved his life, and he felt that everything about her was brave and true, but did he really know her? Gratitude could produce deceptive feelings, and they ought not to be mistaken for more than they were. For the present he would do well to stay as detached as possible. Especially as anxiety hurried the hand and robbed the eye. He was prepared to fight for Grace Tucker — that much he was absolutely sure about — and he would if he got the chance.

Suddenly the dimmest of light gave him back the world he knew, and he found himself in trapped places of the moon. He appeared to have entered an area that was wide and slightly sunken, where the conifers no longer soared high and locked their branches in unbroken ceilings. Here the timber came in shorter, thicker forms and grew less abundantly, and in the background cliffs raised their shadows. There was movement in the air out here, tossing and fitful, and sound too a hinted music that was yet weird and real — for it vibrated softly in elder piping and was accompanied by a low and sinister rattling.

Gunn's right toe kicked a round shape. The object fled short yards before him, knocking like a cracked pot as it spun. He closed upon the shape, seeing it pale against the blackness of the earth, then picked it up and held it towards his eyes, dropping it again almost instantly with a shocked gasp, for he had found himself looking into the eyeless sockets of a bleached human skull.

For long moments he stood trembling, but then he pulled himself together and moved on, ignoring the sounds when his horse bumped the remains of a wooden framework and sent bones showering to the ground. By now he had, of course, realized where he was, and knew that there was nothing in this place to fear but fear itself. He had entered the Indian burial ground of which Grace Tucker had spoken that morning, and the cliffs yonder would contain the caves among which she had believed she might seek a refuge. It was here too, on the probability of things, that the gunbattle had been taking place. But was it over? Had one of the combatants fallen? And if so, which one?

He began angling to his left, aiming to cross the broad hollow and reach the base of the tallest rock in the bluffs opposite him. The weird music kept him company. Its underlying crepitation was now recognisable as sound produced by the strings of shells and rattlesnake rings suspended around the nearby Indian dead. The noise was a form of medicine to protect the occupants of this primitive necropolis from evil spirits, and Gunn now took the utmost care to avoid disturbing any further spot or structures that might be associated with the savage deceased. And he was just about to divert in order to miss another of the wooden catafalques, when a tiny point of fire stabbed at no great distance to his left and a rifle banged within the same split instant.

Crouching, hand upon his six-shooter, Gunn thought that he had been fired upon for a moment; but, hearing no whisper of the bullet, he realized that the shot had actually amounted to a new flare up in the gunbattle that had begun while he was riding the Yellowstone Trail. Then, almost directly after the detonation, there was a new development, for he heard foliage cracking and a man's voice, gruff and triumphant, shout words that sounded like: "Gotcha, you hellcat!"

Gunn left his horse where it stood. Then he launched into a run and headed for the spot where he had seen the flash of the gun; and he had covered a bit more than a hundred yards when he found himself among rocks and scrub timber. Slowing, all his senses at full torsion, he suddenly glimpsed movement ahead of him and made out threshing limbs, the voices of man and woman punctuating the violent exercise with gasps and small snarling voices. Jerking his revolver, Gunn went closer and saw two figures wrestling on the ground, the one on top obviously a broad-backed and very powerful male. Cocking his pistol, he stopped about six feet short of the struggling pair and snapped: "That's enough! Get off her, you varmint!"

The man's shape stiffened briefly; then he rolled to his left and sat up, pistol flaring in his right hand. The bullet fanned Gunn's left cheekbone, causing him to start back sharply, but he blasted a return straight down the line travelled by the first slug and heard a grunt of pain. Then the other's form wobbled blackly erect, looming dangerously, and Gunn fired twice into the middle of it, knowing instinctively that he had made a kill as his target fell like a log. "Grace?" he asked, as the sound of the shots died away and he perceived another human form in the night between him and a large white boulder.

"Yes, Jed," the woman's voice answered shakily.

"Are you all right, girl?" Gunn paused uneasily. "You don't sound it."

"I'm not — quite."

"Been hit?"

"Just now — yes."

"That last shot I heard before I ran here?"

"I expect so."

Holstering his pistol, he stepped up to her, and steadied her into a sitting position on the white rock at her back. "How bad is it, Grace?"

"Not very," she replied. "The bullet passed through the left side of my waist, right at the edge. I'm bleeding fairly, but it isn't much otherwise."

"Will you be able to walk?"

"I think so."

"Then let's get you to one of those caves you told me about. You'll have to show me the way."

"I've already picked one out for myself," she said, "and I've got a fire burning there. I didn't know Dan Striker had been hunting me, until he sprang into my hiding place, but I managed to slide clear of him and then make a fight of it. I thought I had him once — but he proved a little too smart."

"Or, put to it, you were a little too merciful," Gunn suspected, turning aside now and bending over the man whom he had shot. He felt for the throat and the wrist pulses, but the arteries were as still as he had expected, and he turned back to Grace Tucker and went on: "He'll never molest another woman. Figures he had been searching for you through a large piece of the day. I reckon Alec sent him out to find and kill you before the noon hour."

"I imagine my fire helped him find me."

"It would have been wiser if you hadn't lit one," Gunn agreed.

"I thought I was safe."

"Well, it's over now," he observed dismissively. "It's been a better day for us than it's been for the Strikers. Colin, Zebedee — and now Dan — dead. Only Alec's still alive."

"Where is he, Jed?"

"God knows!" Gunn answered. "Though I expect only the devil cares."

"Yes," Grace murmured, "he's as bad as the other three of them put together."

Placing an arm about her, Gunn helped her to her feet; then, after she had indicated that they should move to the left, he steered her away from the boulder and onto open grass. They walked slowly in the direction of the cliffs, Grace holding her left side, and Gunn received the impression that they were rounding the western boundary of the Indian cemetery, for he glimpsed lines of rock and timber which separated the immediate land from places beyond. Their route crossed north and took them along the foot of the mighty wall of stone which now stood on their left, and Grace soon pointed out the tiny smudge of firelight — just above ground level and at the centre of the bluffs — which marked the cave that she had originally picked as her refuge.

They were almost at their goal, when the girl's knees shook a couple of times and almost let her down. Fearing that she might be about to faint from shock and weakness, Gunn lifted her into his arms and carried her up the brief slope before the cave. Then, entering, he laid her down on the thick bed of ferns which she had already made for herself beside a wood fire that was rapidly choking itself under a pile of white ash. "Lie still," he urged. "I'll cheer the fire up. Then we'll have a look at your wound."

"There's plenty of fuel over by the wall," she said, nodding weakly towards the opposite side of the cave.

He found the wood on his left — mostly sear bits and pieces, but some heavier stuff too — and, after a few minutes of fanning handfuls of twigs and dry grass into new flame, and then feeding that flame with fragments of broken boughs, he had a blaze going that cast out real heat and lighted the cavern to an extent that made it possible to see things in some detail.

Grace Tucker had by now taken off her buckskin jacket and pulled out the shirt that she was wearing beneath from the top of her leather trousers, revealing the flesh of her waist and the place on the left where Dan Striker's bullet had pierced it. As she had indicated herself, the wound was well wide of the lower internal organs and very little more than the subcutaneous fat had been broached, but the whiteness of her skin was disfigured by numerous bruises and Gunn got the idea that she had been almost as much hurt by struggling with Dan Striker as she had been by the bullet from his rifle. "You're still bleeding some," Gunn observed. "I'm not sure how much we can do for you. We're not exactly flush with equipment. But I left a horse somewhere across the way. It was Alec Striker's and may be carrying things we can use. I'll go and find it, then bring it back here."

"No," she said. "Don't leave me, please. I don't want to be left alone."

Gunn shrugged. She was suffering from shock — the glassy brightness of her eyes was enough to tell him that — and he reckoned it would be as well to humour her. "I'll bind you up," he said. "This old shirt of mine will stand a bit of tearing."

She didn't argue that, and he pulled off his clothing down to his vest and ripped up the cleanest part of his shirt for bandages. After that he staunched and bandaged up Grace's injury, then helped her dress again. "We can leave here now and head for your cabin if you like," he said. "It isn't all that far, though the woods are dark."

"No," she said. "It's warm here. I want to sleep."

"Whatever you wish," he returned. "I reckon it would be best. You may feel more lively in the morning — though I wouldn't bank on it."

"I'll be all right," she assured him. "Put some more wood on the fire."

He did as she asked, gauging that the fuel she had gathered and laid by would be sufficient to see them through the night; and then he covered her with his jacket and prepared to sit out the dark hours in dozing beside the blaze; but the girl suddenly raised herself a little and said: "Come and hold me, Jed. I want to be held."

"Sure you do," he said, knowing that what she really wanted was to feel safe; and he put his arms around her jacket-wrapped form and held her tightly. "Just till you fall asleep, Grace."

And that was how he intended it should be — for the fire was going

249

to need regular feeding — but lying there, with the white-faced girl sleeping peacefully in his arms, he let the rhythms of life lull him too, and before long he also slept. If he dreamed that night, he was unaware of it, and after a period of storm and stress he lay at peace with all Creation.

It was full morning when he awoke. The events of yesterday seemed far away, and he felt pretty good. The risen sun was filling the gossamer haze outside the cave with a golden glow, and he could hear birds singing. Gently releasing himself from contact with the still sleeping girl, he sat up and yawned, wishing they had some coffee around. Then, almost without shock, he was aware of the presence of a man in the cavemouth who seemed to have appeared on the threshold by magic. "You," he said.

"Me," Alec Striker taunted, holding a cocked revolver between him and the now awakening Grace. "How sweet. Two of you, lying like babes together. I could have plugged you both while you slept, Gunn, but I decided I wanted you both to know it was coming. I've been around here most of the night, and I found Dan and my horse in the light of dawn. The horse is fine, but Dan is dead as the Indians who rot in this cemetery. Pains me that I can't revenge the poor fellow more than once."

"Dead's dead," Gunn agreed. "Be a man, Alec, and spare the girl. She's done you no harm."

"Like hell!" Striker scoffed. "If she hadn't gone and cut you down before you were dead, all three of my brothers would still be alive and kicking. No, I think I'll put a slug between her pretty eyes — and then shoot bits off you. How does that sound?"

"Face me in a fair fight," Gunn challenged. "You're said to be fast on the draw, and I've no reputation."

"Fair fight!" Striker hooted. "That honour thing never did touch me. Why, you might win, Jed. I want you dead, and I don't care how. Where does honour stand in that?"

"You contemptible scum!" Gunn spat.

Striker's revolver boomed, and Gunn's heart almost stopped as the girl beside him, now raised into a sitting position, cried out; but a quick glance to his left revealed that she was unharmed, except for the loss of a blonde tress which had just been shot away from her left temple.

Gunn felt compelled to try it. Rolling onto his left buttock, he grabbed for his Colt, but the weapon had no sooner cleared leather than Striker shot it out of his grasp and it went clattering into the back of the cave.

"Not bad," Striker observed. "I could beat you to the draw okay, but why live on the difference?" He laughed coldly and cynically. "I knew you were behind me last night, mister. I got the ear, and I reckoned to lay for you. But that shooting out here caused you to turn aside. Saved your life for then." Now he licked his lips, gloating fiendishly.

"Well, we've had our moments, eh? Now let's get the dying done — so I can get on up to Montana and spend some of that bank money I stole." He slowly cocked his gun again. "Like to kiss the girl farewell, Jed? You can — after I've spoiled her face!"

Gunn watched helplessly, lost in horror, as Striker raised his Colt and took deliberate aim at the blonde's brow. Then man's finger began to squeeze the trigger, tendons hardening into view and flesh whitening. Then once again the pistol roared, yet something happened in that instant, for the bullet went high as Striker's body gave a violent jerk. Now he stood there, a bewildered expression on his face, and all at once he toppled forward and measured his length into the cave. It was now revealed that there was a black arrow driven deep between his shoulder-blades.

Thrusting himself to his feet, Gunn sprang into the mouth of the cave and looked out into the morning haze. The person who had brought about Alec

Striker's end ought to be still in sight, but the ground before him was empty. He could see only the trees and the sun-stained mists that hovered among them in the windless day. There was no sign of life anywhere.

"Was it Roaring Bear?" Grace inquired.

"Like as not," Gunn said, hiding the doubt in his eye. "That's a Blackfoot war arrow anyhow, and it was surely, loosed from the bow of a friend. You live, Miss Tucker, and so do I. Perhaps we're met here for a purpose."

"What could that be, Jed?"

"You know very well," he answered. "We're two of a kind, and I guess it's up to us to make whatever there is to be. How do you feel about cows?"

"I can take them or leave them."

"That about covers it for me too," he admitted. "But it's a beginning of sorts, because we've got a ranch to run." He saw her starting to rise. "No, no — stay there, Grace. I reckon I'll find a couple of horses nearby. They'll take us home." She was looking at him strangely now, and he gave her a lopsided grin and added: "The ranch house needs some work done on it. Still, I daresay you'll turn out to be a dab hand with a paint brush."

He left the cave, nodding to himself. The material was there; it was up to them how they shaped it. And he must look up old Roaring Bear sometime. Any friend of Grace Tucker's was now a friend of his.

THE END

FIGHTING RAMROD
Charles N. Heckelmann

Most men would have cut their losses, but Frazer counted the bullets in his guns and said he'd soak the range in blood before he'd give up another inch of what was his.

LONE GUN
Eric Allen

Smoke Blackbird had been away too long. The Lequires had seized the Blackbird farm, forcing the Indians and settlers off, and no one seemed willing to fight! He had to fight alone.

THE THIRD RIDER
Barry Cord

Mel Rawlins wasn't going to let anything stand in his way. His father was murdered, his two brothers gone. Now Mel rode for vengeance.

ARIZONA DRIFTERS
W. C. Tuttle

When drifting Dutton and Lonnie Steelman decide to become partners they find that they have a common enemy in the formidable Thurston brothers.

TOMBSTONE
Matt Braun

Wells Fargo paid Luke Starbuck to outgun the silver-thieving stagecoach gang at Tombstone. Before long Luke can see the only thing bearing fruit in this eldorado will be the gallows tree.

HIGH BORDER RIDERS
Lee Floren

Buckshot McKee and Tortilla Joe cut the trail of a border tough who was running Mexican beef into Texas. They stopped the smuggler in his tracks.

BRETT RANDALL, GAMBLER
E. B. Mann

Larry Day had the choice of running away from the law or of assuming a dead man's place. No matter what he decided he was bound to end up dead.

THE GUNSHARP
William R. Cox

The Eggerleys weren't very smart. They trained their sights on Will Carney and Arizona's biggest blood bath began.

THE DEPUTY OF SAN RIANO
Lawrence A. Keating and
Al. P. Nelson

When a man fell dead from his horse, Ed Grant was spotted riding away from the scene. The deputy sheriff rode out after him and came up against everything from gunfire to dynamite.

FARGO: MASSACRE RIVER
John Benteen

The ambushers up ahead had now blocked the road. Fargo's convoy was a jumble, a perfect target for the insurgents' weapons!

SUNDANCE: DEATH IN THE LAVA
John Benteen

The Modoc's captured the wagon train and its cargo of gold. But now the halfbreed they called Sundance was going after it . . .

HARSH RECKONING
Phil Ketchum

Five years of keeping himself alive in a brutal prison had made Brand tough and careless about who he gunned down . . .

FARGO: PANAMA GOLD
John Benteen

With foreign money behind him, Buckner was going to destroy the Panama Canal before it could be completed. Fargo's job was to stop Buckner.

FARGO: THE SHARPSHOOTERS
John Benteen

The Canfield clan, thirty strong were raising hell in Texas. Fargo was tough enough to hold his own against the whole clan.

PISTOL LAW
Paul Evan Lehman

Lance Jones came back to Mustang for just one thing — revenge! Revenge on the people who had him thrown in jail.

HELL RIDERS
Steve Mensing

Wade Walker's kid brother, Duane, was locked up in the Silver City jail facing a rope at dawn. Wade was a ruthless outlaw, but he was smart, and he had vowed to have his brother out of jail before morning!

DESERT OF THE DAMNED
Nelson Nye

The law was after him for the murder of a marshal — a murder he didn't commit. Breen was after him for revenge — and Breen wouldn't stop at anything . . . blackmail, a frameup . . . or murder.

DAY OF THE COMANCHEROS
Steven C. Lawrence

Their very name struck terror into men's hearts — the Comancheros, a savage army of cutthroats who swept across Texas, leaving behind a blood-stained trail of robbery and murder.

SUNDANCE: SILENT ENEMY
John Benteen

A lone crazed Cheyenne was on a personal war path. They needed to pit one man against one crazed Indian. That man was Sundance.

LASSITER
Jack Slade

Lassiter wasn't the kind of man to listen to reason. Cross him once and he'll hold a grudge for years to come — if he let you live that long.

LAST STAGE TO GOMORRAH
Barry Cord

Jeff Carter, tough ex-riverboat gambler, now had himself a horse ranch that kept him free from gunfights and card games. Until Sturvesant of Wells Fargo showed up.

McALLISTER
ON THE
COMANCHE CROSSING
Matt Chisholm

The Comanche, McAllister owes them a life — and the trail is soaked with the blood of the men who had tried to outrun them before.

QUICK-TRIGGER COUNTRY
Clem Colt

Turkey Red hooked up with Curly Bill Graham's outlaw crew. But wholesale murder was out of Turk's line, so when range war flared he bucked the whole border gang alone . . .

CAMPAIGNING
Jim Miller

Ambushed on the Santa Fe trail, Sean Callahan is saved by two Indian strangers. But there'll be more lead and arrows flying before the band join Kit Carson against the Comanches.

GUNSLINGER'S RANGE
Jackson Cole

Three escaped convicts are out for revenge. They won't rest until they put a bullet through the head of the dirty snake who locked them behind bars.

RUSTLER'S TRAIL
Lee Floren

Jim Carlin knew he would have to stand up and fight because he had staked his claim right in the middle of Big Ike Outland's best grass.

THE TRUTH ABOUT SNAKE RIDGE
Marshall Grover

The troubleshooters came to San Cristobal to help the needy. For Larry and Stretch the turmoil began with a brawl and then an ambush.

WOLF DOG RANGE
Lee Floren

Will Ardery would stop at nothing, unless something stopped him first — like a bullet from Pete Manly's gun.

DEVIL'S DINERO
Marshall Grover

Plagued by remorse, a rich old reprobate hired the Texas Troubleshooters to deliver a fortune in greenbacks to each of his victims.

GUNS OF FURY
Ernest Haycox

Dane Starr, alias Dan Smith, wanted to close the door on his past and hang up his guns, but people wouldn't let him.